MISSION:
VAQUITA

MISSION: VAQUITA

S. H. GOODHART

for Michael

"And maybe Mother Earth will produce a great being sometime in the next decade... We don't know and we cannot predict. Mother Earth is very talented. She has produced Buddhas, bodhisattvas, great beings."

Thich Nhat Hanh

I am one of the last of my tribe.
They took my wife. They took my daughter. They took my sons.
Why am I still here?
Is there any who will hear the history of my tribe? So that we may live on, in legend if nothing else?
My bones are old and I ache when I swim.
Since I know the madness will not stop, all I can do is try to watch over my brethren. And hope for a messenger who will tell of us, the vaquitas. I no longer believe any can save us. But perhaps one will tell our story.

El Jefe

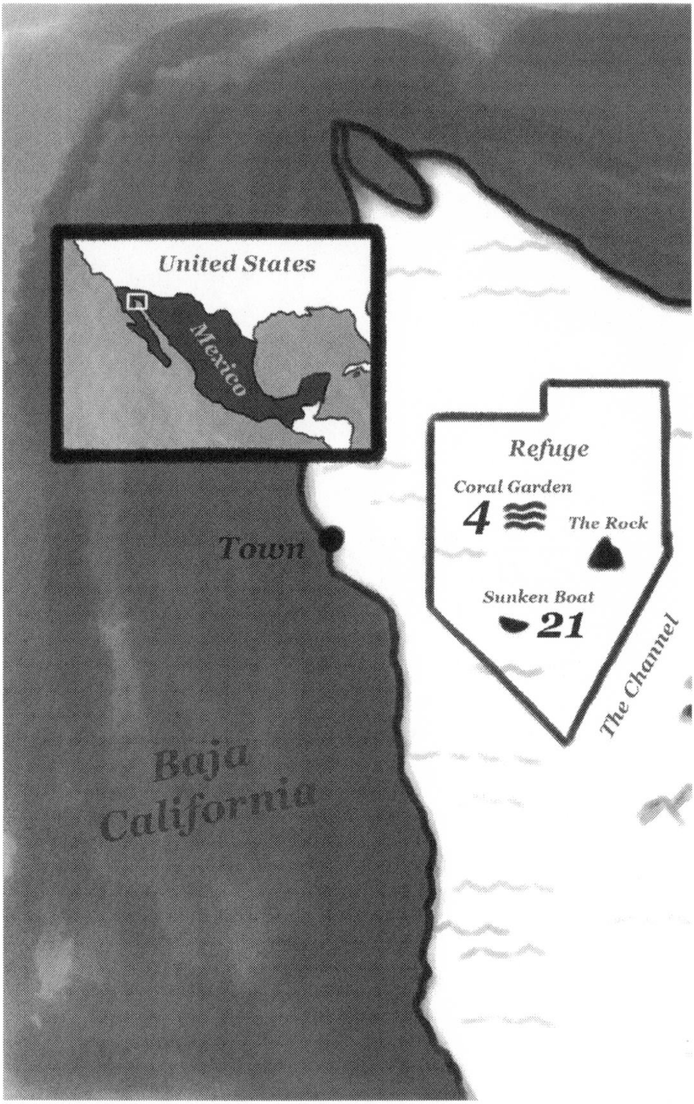
United States
Mexico
Refuge
Coral Garden
4
The Rock
Sunken Boat
21
The Channel
Town
Baja
California

Where the Vaquitas Are

Sonora

Area **8**

Kelp Forest

The Summit

Sea of Cortez

PART I: ANITA ALONE

That night, she learns what not to do. After cutting away, she's made no progress at all. The plastic mesh is too dense. "I'll have to think of another way," Anita says to herself, strapping the bowie knife back to her thigh. Exhausted, she swims slowly back to the beach.

The work is a labor of love. She's never even seen a vaquita. But this is their home, as much as it is hers.

She emerges on the sand, utterly dejected. Her great idea was a failure. Time is running out.

* * * * * * *

Thirty left. Only thirty. Just a year ago, the estimate was sixty. "How can this be happening?" Anita cries aloud, the stars her only audience.

She knows the answer: greed. Humans are killing vaquitas off for money. Not on purpose – no, their real target is the totoaba. The totoaba fish is more valuable than cocaine. The nets that catch the fish also trap the vaquitas.

Trudging home through the dark streets, she wonders, "What can I do?" But the Milky Way doesn't answer.

* * * * * * * *

Anita slips back into her parents' small house. Their dog doesn't bark. "Thank goodness for you, Coco," she whispers, petting his light brown head. Inside her tiny room, she removes the wetsuit, pulls a nightshirt over her damp skin, and crawls into bed.

She catches a few hours of sleep before the alarm rings. Getting dressed, her mind returns to last night's failure. She sighs and goes to the kitchen for a quick breakfast. "What can I do?" she demands, but her cereal doesn't answer.

She's just finished eating when her father enters the room. "Good morning, Papá."

Miguel hugs his daughter, and the hug seems tighter than usual, almost as if he's holding on. Anita knows he's been having a tough time lately. Fishing is all he's ever known.

"How do you like being a man of leisure?" she asks, trying to keep it light.

"It's not too bad, Tita. I'm going to start painting the house today. I'll make it look nice for you and your mother. She chose a bright blue: 'to go with...'"

"'...our sea'!" Anita laughs, finishing her mother's words.

She hugs him again, then leaves. She heads to her mother's taquería on the malecón, the promenade along the shore. Villagers greet her as she walks: "¡Buenos días, Tita!" and "There's our Little Fish!" They've known her since she was born. She waves and gives a weak smile.

It's just past 8:00 but the June sun is already showing its strength. Anita pulls her long dark hair into a pony tail. "It's going to be a hot one," she says, greeting her mother, and squeezing past her to take position in the kitchen.

María looks out at the patio, already flooded with sunlight, and says, "Yes, the beach should be busy. Let's get to it." She hands her daughter a sack of onions.

2

Anita's mind wanders as she chops. "Chopping all day, chopping all night... I'm having much better luck with these onions than with that net. If cutting the nets down won't work... what can I do?"

* * * * * * * *

The customers begin to arrive. It's a mixed bunch of locals, tourists. And these days, scientists and government officials. Anita's nice to everyone but somewhat cool to the officials. What have they done to this point? The animals are disappearing under their watch.

As Anita walks over to a table, her right wrist begins to ache, a deep gnawing pain. She shakes it out for some relief, then asks the man for his order. She notices his hat says Sea Shepherd.

"On our side," she thinks, then summons the courage to ask him a question. In her intermediate-level English, she asks, "You are here... to patrol the waters?"

"That's right," he says, smiling. But it's not a very convincing smile. Clearly, he's worried, too.

"Have you seen any vaquitas?" Anita asks, not sure she wants to know the answer.

His face breaks into a wide, genuine smile. "I saw my first one yesterday!"

So they really do exist! She walks to the kitchen, relief flooding her. Relief and an idea.

"I'll be a shepherd. A vaquita shepherd!"

* * * * * * * *

A YOUNG ADULT FEMALE VAQUITA

I come from a beautiful place. I wish I could show it to you. If I could, I'm sure you would want to protect it.

My own powers are limited. I can swim and I can care for

3

young vaquis. I cared for my sister after our mother died, drowned in the sea which gives us life.

It is a strange thing, the drowning of us porpoises. I don't understand it. The water is everything to us. But there is a trap, a swallowing something that makes it so we cannot rise to the surface and breathe.

I am shy and do not venture close to the shore. But I have seen the humans on their rafts. My friend tells me they bring the darkness that suffocated my mother. El Jefe says this, too. I don't understand what they mean.

I am simple. We vaquitas do not school. El Jefe says it is because of what happened during the Orca Times. Since then, we do not swim together.

In separation, for many thousands of moons, we were safe. But not educated.

Now we are not educated and we are not safe.

Still, I know where there is a beautiful garden. I would be happy to show it to you.

* * * * * * * *

Anita loves her parents and enjoys them. But tonight all she thinks is, "Can't they go to sleep? I have to find my flock!"

At long last, their TV program ends, and she hears them getting ready for bed. When she's sure they're settled, she pulls her wetsuit on as quietly as she can. Coco sits staring at her. He likes to watch this silly game, his Tita struggling to get into the funny skin.

The damp neoprene fights her at every turn, but finally the suit is on. She straps a flashlight and her knife to her thigh, then pads out of her room.

4

Coco follows her to the door. He gives her a look that says, "You're a bit crazy, but I love you, and I won't tell on you."

Their home is a five minute walk to the beach. It's a moonless night and Anita passes unnoticed through the dark town, her eyes taking in as much as they can. In the homes she passes, there's no visible activity, just a few glowing TVs.

Tonight the beach is empty. "Perfect," she thinks. "Less explaining to do." Anita heads into the warm water. If her swimming were brief, she wouldn't need a wetsuit.

She dips her head into the Sea of Cortez. Her first strokes are light and easy, her head coming up between them in case anyone is near. When she's confident she's past being seen, she dives underwater and propels herself like a torpedo.

There's ground to cover tonight. Sea to cover.

She races ten miles, never stopping for breath, never needing to stop for breath. It's been three years since the change occurred. The novelty's gone, but still there are times she can't believe it.

* * * * * * *

Now at sixteen, Anita is small. When she was thirteen, she was tiny. Tiny but fast.

And one Sunday back then, there was a big family picnic on the beach. While some of the cousins started a volleyball game, her cousin Pablo decided a different contest was in order.

"Tita, I'll race you to the lighthouse!" Even as he said it, Pablo was dashing down the sand to get a head start.

"No fair!" she yelled. "Pablo's cheating, everybody!" She tore down the beach after him and dove into the water.

The teenagers interrupted their volleyball game, the children abandoned their sand castles, and the adults left the grill. Everyone ran down to the shore. Pablo was two years older and four inches taller than Anita, but no one had ever heard of her losing a swimming contest.

With their families cheering them on, the two fought each other and the waves. At the very end, Anita pulled ahead, to the delight of the littlest cousins.

Emerging on the beach, she could barely hear the congratulations over the din of her own thoughts. "What just happened?! Did I imagine it?... Did anyone notice?" She looked at the smiling faces, and saw only the usual affection and pride. No one in her family had noticed. The whitecaps had obscured her movements.

But down the beach, a tall woman stood, her curly hair blowing in the wind. Her brown eyes were as sharp as a hawk's. She had witnessed it all, and knew: something special was in the water.

Anita was too flustered to notice the woman. All she could think was, "I have to go out tonight. I have to see for sure."

That evening was the first time she snuck out of the house. As he always did when the family left him, Coco barked as she departed. She turned and looked into his eyes and said, "No, Coco."

He never barked at her again.

That night, she confirmed it: she could swim without coming up for air.

* * * * * * * *

The swimming ability came all at once; what took longer was the vision. But slowly, Anita's eyes changed, and now she can see as a fish does. Instead of dark murky waters, the sea is alive with fluorescence.

Searching for her flock, sixteen year-old Anita is now deep in the Refuge – the protected vaquita area. She's paddling about, looking for the elusive creatures, when a school of neon-blue fish appears. Noticing her and recognizing her as an old friend, they come to a stop. Then, as a greeting, they perform an elaborate figure eight. Their light is strong.

Anita tells them, "Hello! Thanks for being here. It's much

easier to see when you're around!" She says this without speaking, her thoughts conveyed telepathically through the water.

The fish are happy to help. They swim near her for ten minutes, glowing as she looks for vaquitas. But when they suddenly sense something in the water, something unpleasant, they abruptly switch off their light and dart away.

Left in darkness, Anita is about to turn on her flashlight when she feels it, a perturbation in the water. "That can only mean one thing," she thinks, breaking into a smile. She surfaces and yells, "Mateo!"

Hearing her, the orca stops. He turns his enormous body towards her, and then he breaches with joy. As he crashes back into the water, he sends a shower of water in all directions.

Laughing as the droplets hit her, Anita calls, "You scared the fish!" She rushes towards her friend. Reaching him, Anita puts her arm out to embrace as much of his huge flank as she can. They hug each other at the surface and enjoy the stars together for a moment.

Then Mateo gives a series of clicks: "Where were you last night?"

"I'm sorry I didn't meet you. I just learned about a new vaquita survey and it upset me."

The whale hangs motionless in the water, his massive silence encouraging her to explain.

"They say there are only about thirty vaquitas left. So I decided to cut down nets... but it didn't work."

Mateo clicks, trying to comfort her. Then he tilts his body, offering his back for a ride.

She shakes her head. "I can't play tonight, Mateo. I must find the vaquitas. Do you know where any are? Do you ever see them?"

Hesitating, Mateo finally clicks, "There are some nearby, in the Garden."

The Garden? Anita knows these waters well, but never heard of such a place. "Where is that, Mateo? Can you show me?"

The orca's clicks take on a deeper, sadder tone. "It's not far." His head turns slightly to the left, indicating the direction. "But I can't take you. The vaquitas fear me. I don't want to scare them."

Suddenly Anita understands. Vaquitas are rare, but that's not the only reason why she never sees them. It's because she swims with Mateo. He avoids their areas, and the vaquitas avoid him.

As this knowledge hits her, Mateo does something brave. The orca turns, and with slowly building speed, he starts racing away from her.

A lump forms in Anita's throat. "Thank you, Mateo," she calls, her eyes tearing up. "I'll see you again."

* * * * * * * *

EL JEFE

I made my rounds today. It was with a heavy heart, as yesterday I heard that Ceti was missing. Today I had to break the news to his brother: a turtle I know saw Ceti gathered into a pile with many other creatures and lifted from our sea.

Our numbers grow smaller.

My counting is poor, but I have done the figures over and over. With Ceti gone, I believe there are thirty-six of us left.

I have no hunger and will go to sleep without feeding. It is hard to go on. I often feel these days that I would prefer not waking up.

It is not right, to see the disappearance of one's kind. If I could strike a blow at the humans, I would. But we vaquitas are peaceful. And powerless.

* * * * * * * *

Mateo is gone. Anita immediately turns left, swimming fast. She notices that the familiar bare sandy bottom starts to show a pale coral here and there. She swims a long time, and all she sees are sparse patches of sickly reef.

"Is this the Garden? It's terrible!" If she could sigh underwater, she would. She's heard that corals are struggling all over the world. Seeing it here with her own eyes is painful.

But her mind returns to her task: will she see a vaquita? "They're very shy," Anita tells herself. She tries to ignore the obvious: they're disappearing.

She keeps her eyes peeled, looking for them, looking for nets. "And looking for fishermen." She shudders at the notion. Somewhere, out in the expanse of sea, outlaws are putting up nets. What will she do if she encounters them?

The night wears on. Sometimes it's just blackness facing her. Other times, fish fluoresce or plankton emit light. But overall it's a dark and lonely mission.

Her spirits low, Anita heads home. She knows she'll come out the next night. It might be futile, but she has to try.

* * * * * * * *

Anita sleeps for two hours before the alarm jolts her awake. Time to go to work. "Too early," she murmurs into her pillow, then forces herself up and out of the house.

She's already feeling down; when Sr. Jiménez comes to the stand, her heart sinks. She's never liked her father's old fishing partner.

María greets him, bringing him a free coffee. Anita doesn't think her mother likes him much, either, but she always says, "We should be grateful to him, he took your father on when he was just a young man."

Anita calls hello from the back and throws him a half-hearted smile. She stays put, dicing tomatoes.

María takes a break from the lunch preparations and chats with him. "How are you, José?"

"Bah... the money is not as good as when we would fish

9

the shrimp..."

"Yes, but it's not bad... and it's good for your backs to have a break. Besides, I don't want us to lose the vaquita..."

"Or the totoaba!" Anita calls out. She feels badly for the totoaba. It isn't good-looking and its claim to fame is something disgustingly called a "swim bladder." But it's facing extinction, too.

"Right. Or the totoaba," says María.

Sr. Jiménez barely listens and just says, "I don't even think vaquitas exist anymore. I saw them when I was twenty... now I am sixty. Forty years without seeing one? Bah!"

He reaches for his coffee and drinks it down, as if to say, "And that's the final word about that!"

He thanks María and says goodbye to them both.

Once he's gone, Anita turns to her mother and says, "I know vaquitas are still out there. Sea Shepherd saw them…"

"Yes, yes, Anita," cuts in her mother. "He is just an unhappy man. His world is changing and he doesn't know what to do."

* * * * * * * *

The work day winds down. Anita is considering how she can find the vaquitas when María says, "Tita, I need to go to the market. Will you close up?"

"Of course, Mamá."

Anita starts to clean the kitchen. As she's putting food away, she hears a customer out front, and irritation rises. Why do people always come at the worst time? Isn't it obvious she's closing?

"Be right there!" she calls out, hoping her voice sounds friendly. She puts away a bowl of peppers, and as she does so, an electric shock stabs her right wrist.

"What did I do to it?" she wonders. "Did I hurt it swimming?"

Irritated by the late customer and irritated by pain, she walks forward, head down, announcing, "The kitchen is closed,

I'm afraid."

"I just wanted a coffee, is that ok? I have a long night ahead of me."

Anita finally looks up, and into the regal face of a tall woman with a crown of curly dark hair.

Anita is shy, yes. But not normally tongue-tied. She doesn't understand why nothing comes out of her mouth. All she can do is feel herself staring at this woman. Is it because she's beautiful? Maybe. She is very beautiful, after all. But, no, that's not it. Anita feels she knows her.

Finally Anita stammers, "Um... yes, we have coffee... but it's pretty old..."

"That's ok. I'm used to drinking bad coffee." The woman's brown eyes are warm, and full of laughter and affection. But isn't affection usually for someone you know?

Anita struggles to place this person. Has she been to the restaurant before? Maybe that's it. But she'd remember someone like that! She manages to ask, "Why are you used to bad coffee?"

"I'm a marine biologist. Sometimes I go on long research trips. There's usually just a small crew. We all take turns at watch... a lot of coffee gets made... and a lot of coffee sits around!"

She laughs and the sound is deep and soothing. There's a lot of wisdom in that laugh, Anita thinks. Then wonders where an idea like that came from. Wisdom?!

In a bit of mental turmoil, Anita turns to business to steady herself. She goes to get the coffee pot. Though her arm aches carrying it, she manages to pour a cup without spilling any.

The woman takes the cup and puts it down. Extending her hand, she says, "I'm Dr. Yolanda Rios."

Dr. Yolanda Rios! That's who she is! Of course! How could Anita forget? Her photo had been in the paper many times. She was the lead scientist on the vaquita conservation efforts.

Anita gushes, "You came up with the payment scheme!"

Dr. Rios jokes, "Shhh... you might want to be a little quiet about that. I'm not sure I'm that popular around here... I hear there have been some problems with it. Not all the fishermen are happy about it."

"My father gets the payments. He misses fishing, but he and my mother agree it's the right thing to do."

Dr. Rios nods and says, "Miguel Pérez was the first to sign up."

Anita's mind reels. She knows who my father is?

"He understood that we had to make the Refuge bigger. The protected area was too small before. It wasn't working. The vaquitas were dying too quickly."

She adds, "Of course, the legal fishermen were only a small part of it. It's the poachers who are the real problem... and they're still out there, still using illegal nets. Laws don't matter unless the laws are enforced... and corruption makes that hard. The animals are up against it, I'm afraid."

It's a somber note, but Anita is pleased that Dr. Rios is talking to her like an adult. "Did you always study vaquitas?" she asks.

"No, my PhD was on swim bladders – do you know what those are?"

Anita nods: Of course. She's a fisherman's daughter. "Fish use the bladders to control how they float. And where they go."

"Right! Well, the totoaba was my main subject. Have you ever seen a totoaba?"

"Only dead on the beach."

Dr. Rios shakes her head in dismay, "It's awful. A long time ago, people caught them for food. But now that fishing totoaba is illegal, no one wants to be caught with the bodies, so they just take the bladders and waste the rest..." She pauses briefly and stares at her coffee, and Anita senses she's stumbling over the foolishness of people.

Then she resumes her story: "Of course, you can't study totoaba without learning of the vaquita. Being a fish researcher, I didn't know much about porpoises... but it didn't take me long to fall in love with those little guys."

Anita smiles. In pictures, vaquitas were cute. Easy to love.

With increased emotion, the scientist continues, "All this death for nothing! Eastern medicine has a lot to offer... but not this! Ground fish bladder as a cure for... you name it! Wrinkles, knee pain, their kids not visiting. It's absurd! Unless we can end that trade, the vaquitas and the totoaba are in big trouble."

She takes a few sips of coffee and a worried silence settles over them both. Then she asks, "And what about you, Tita?"

Anita's mind reels again. She knows my nickname? The she answers, "I... hope to stay here, and work with my mother. I don't want to leave my family... or our sea."

Dr. Rios nods and says, "It's good to love your home." She finishes the coffee and leaves.

* * * * * * *

Walking home, Anita looks ahead to her swim. She wants to be optimistic – she has a path in mind to try to find the Garden – but she feels upset. People in her town are causing the vaquitas' destruction. Maybe even people she knows.

She tries to be sympathetic. "I know it can be hard to make a living here."

But for quack medicine? For people thousands of miles away?

"I need a swim to clear my mind." She almost aches to get in the sea.

* * * * * * *

COCO

My master has always been Miguel Pérez. It took me a long time to learn his name but it took me no time at all to learn he was my master. He saved me from the streets, finding me and my mother in a garbage bin. With his wife and young daughter, Miguel cared for us, trying hard to get my mother well. But she died soon after he found us, too thirsty and weak after so much time giving herself for me.

Miguel buried her deep in the sandy soil behind our house. I visit the spot every day and tell my mother I am fine. I tell her I have a good home.

I learned he is called "Miguel" because his wife says his name so much. She is very nice but she orders him around a little bit. "Miguel, don't forget to put gas in the car." "Miguel, be careful when you fish today." Or my favorite, "Miguel, don't forget to get food for Coco." Hearing this makes me happy. But I know Miguel would never forget to get food for me.

The girl was very tiny when I came. I was tiny, too, so we were well matched. For a long time we were the same size but now she is bigger than me. I don't mind.

When she started school, I tried to help her with her work. I was not very good at it – I wanted to chew the papers, which I could tell her unhappy. But together we learned her name: Anita Pérez, or Tita for short. With her, I even learned some numbers that had to do with the telephone device. Numbers to keep her safe if she was ever lost. But I would never let her become lost and so I have forgotten them.

We used to play in the sea together. Such happy times. But she no longer wants to do this with me. I do not understand why. I know she still enters the sea because I can smell it on her.

Tonight Tita said to me, as she slipped out again, "Coco, my love, I'll be back soon. Don't you worry."

I am not worried about her. I know she will be safe. And so I do not bark.

But I am a little worried about me. Am I being disloyal to my master Miguel? I do not know if he wants her to leave the house every night.

* * * * * * * *

After a distracted dinner with her parents, and after waiting what seemed like years for them to go to bed, Anita is finally in her sea. She returns to the place where she and Mateo separated last night. This time, she swims a little farther before she follows his instruction to turn left. Soon, she's rewarded: a magnificent field of corals surrounds her, not the pale dying plants of yesterday, but healthy lush reefs. Astonished, Anita tries to take all the colors in: reds and oranges of every hue, shocking pinks and purples. Striped fish, even more gorgeous than the corals, dart among the fanning plants.

"This is so beautiful!" She almost wants to cry she's so relieved.

Then she turns her head and notices someone else enjoying the garden: Vaquita!

Anita's chest feels like it's going to explode. There it is, a vaquita nibbling at the coral. Wait... there's another one... and another! Three vaquitas, about ten feet away!

By the corals' glow, Anita gazes at the porpoises with delight. Delight that they exist. Delight at their goofy faces, with dark circles around their eyes and dark lipsticked mouths. They look like little girls who got into their mothers' make-up cases.

"Thank you, Universe," Anita says, as her eyes eagerly take them in. She's surprised how little they are – even smaller than she is. "It's hard to believe you're relatives of whales!"

Anita recalls what she's read: female vaquitas are usually bigger than males. So she realizes she's seeing one female and two males. The smallest one must still be a child.

Underwater, the vaquitas stare at her with as much awe as she stares at them. Nobody moves. Anita can barely register all the emotions flooding her: joy, excitement, anxiety, awe. She concentrates on sending out loving thoughts, on telling the

15

vaquitas she's their friend.

She can't tell if it's reaching them, but they're clearly fascinated by her. In fact, if it weren't necessary for them to breathe, the vaquitas might gawk at Anita all night. But breathe they must, so after a few moments they break their gaze and head to the surface. Anita follows them up.

The porpoises exhale through their blowholes, and Anita takes it as her moment. She announces, "I'm here to help you."

The three buzz at one another. Then the female – the first one she saw – inches towards Anita. The males edge closer too.

Anita explains, "I will swim with you and keep you safe."

The leader is now within touching distance. Has Anita's heart stopped? She's pretty sure it has.

Anita doesn't move; even the water is still. Slowly, the leader advances, and then very gingerly she touches Anita's hand with her snout. Anita will never forget that sensation, the smooth porpoise skin brushing against her flesh.

The vaquita lifts her head, and clicks excitedly to the others. Their little doll-like faces seem to break into smiles. Soon all three are surrounding Anita, and nuzzling her arms.

* * * * * * * *

Anita swims as if in a dream. She's found them! And they trust her! Her idea wasn't so crazy, after all. She giggles, "'Vaquita' means 'little cow'... so of course they need a shepherd!"

Giddiness makes her want to laugh out loud. Then she realizes she's in front. "Why am I leading them? They should lead me!"

She stops and the three porpoises stop, too. She says, "You show me where to go, and I'll follow."

The leader – by this time, Anita's named her Esperanza (Hope) – turns to her pod. The animals begin swimming, turning to make sure Anita follows.

Anita barely registers the seascape as she follows her

16

friends. Though they leave the Garden, everything still looks beautiful to her. She spends the next few hours in pure elation.

Eventually, sadly, Anita knows she has to go. "But what will happen to them while I'm gone?" She saw no nets tonight, but they only swam in a tiny portion of the vaquitas' range.

She tells them: "I have to leave you now. Try to stay in the areas we visited together. I'll come tomorrow and meet you at the Coral Garden. Where we first met."

The three porpoises come up and nuzzle her arms again. "Goodbye for now, little cows," she says, then torpedoes off.

* * * * * * * *

EL JEFE

My grief over Ceti continues... and, yet... tonight I felt something in the water, a vibration I have not experienced since childhood. A lifting of the heaviness. Dare I say it? A joyful peace.

Is something good happening, or is this just the Sun and Sea Creator preparing me for the Infinite Sea? I suspect I will go there soon.

* * * * * * * *

Anita's heart is so full she wonders if it might break. "I never knew happiness could break your heart..." she muses as she wrings out her hair.

On the beach at 3:00 a.m., Anita thinks she's alone. She breaks into a dance. "I met the vaquitas! I met the vaquitas!" she giggles and laughs and leaps on the sand. Her joy is so full she doesn't even notice her right wrist is aching again.

"I will protect them!" she cries to the heavens. "They will not die out on my watch!"

Knowing she has to get back, she grabs her shoes from the seawall and rushes towards home.

Down the beach, shrouded in darkness, Yolanda Rios watches Anita leave.

* * * * * * *

The next day Anita feels so light that her feet barely touch the ground. "I can swim like a fish... who knows, maybe I can fly like a bird!" She looks down and checks: her feet are firmly on the floor. More reality: her mother says, "Tita, do you mind closing up again?"

"Of course not, Mamá."

Anita goes out to clear dishes from the patio. She lets the sun shine on her face for a moment, and imagines seeing Espy and the other two that night. "Maybe they can introduce me to more vaquitas!" Then she turns to a table and begins stacking dirty dishes. The pain in her right wrist comes and is almost unbearable.

"Tita."

The girl spins around to face the voice. "Oh, Dr. Rios. Hello! Do you want some coffee?"

"Not this time, Tita. I've come to talk to you."

Anita looks at her blankly. Confusion reigns at first... and then an inkling rises in her.

"Tell me, Tita... is your right wrist hurting?"

Time stops for Anita, and her ears ring with the question. Finally, she murmurs, "How did you know?"

"I've been watching you, Tita. Over the years, I've been watching you. I was there, the day you raced that boy to the lighthouse. You're no ordinary swimmer."

* * * * * * *

"The lighthouse?" Anita asks... or does she squeak? It feels to her like she squeaks. A little mouse scared of a cat. A girl scared of the tiger of her life.

"I watched you. I'm sure that was the day you discovered your gift... in fact, I followed you that night. You went back out for a swim... like you were proving it to yourself."

Anita can barely believe her ears. Yolanda has known about me for three years?! Still mouse-like, she says nothing.

"And last night?" Yolanda asks.

The mouse disappears, and Anita finds herself almost defiant. "I found the vaquitas. I found them."

"Yes, I thought so… Tita, I'll leave now so you can work. But I want to show you something. Will you meet me at your beach at midnight?"

Flustered and excited, Anita nods. Then she asks, "Dr. Rios... how did you know about my wrist?"

"Call me Yolanda. And I'll tell you tonight."

* * * * * * * *

Anita doesn't know what to think or feel. She's thrilled she'll see the vaquitas again. And she's excited over what Yolanda will show her. But scared, too. And what if Yolanda takes all night? Will the vaquitas worry if she doesn't come? What if they get hurt?!

On an emotional roller-coaster, she manages to get through dinner somehow. Then she fakes it through the evening with her parents; their favorite TV show is on, so that helps. No need for her to talk.

The show ends and they all get ready to sleep. "Good night, Little Fish," her father says, heading to bed.

"'Night, Papá." Anita hopes this sounds normal.

Her mother is right beside her. Is it her imagination, or is her mother lingering?

"Well, good night, Mamá…"

María's eyes search her daughter's face. Uncomfortable, Anita looks to the floor. Then she gives a little laugh, and wills herself to look up at her mother.

Their brown eyes meet. Anita concentrates on holding the gaze, hoping whatever she conveys will satisfy her mother.

At long last, María turns away. "Goodnight, Tita," she says, then goes to the bedroom to join Miguel.

With relief, Anita retreats to her own room. Waiting in there, Anita can't hear her parents' conversation, but we can: María starts off, "Tita's so quiet these days. I'm worried about her. She never sees her friends anymore."

"I know. But she's always had a quiet side. And she did well in school this year, as usual."

"But what about swimming? She always loved that, Miguel, and now she never goes."

"I think our Tita swims after work. There are always towels in the laundry..." Tired, they leave off their discussion and kiss each other goodnight.

They fall asleep quickly. Miguel's snoring is so loud tonight that Anita doesn't even have to put her head against the wall to hear it. She gets her wetsuit on and heads out.

* * * * * * * *

Reaching the beach, Anita finds Yolanda sitting on the wall. The woman is in a tank suit.

Yolanda stands up. "I thought we could swim together, Tita."

Anita nods, as if caught in a spell. She senses what's ahead.

The two walk down to the water. Without words and without looking at Anita, Yolanda dives into the waves. The girl follows.

The sea draws them to itself; deeper and deeper it pulls them in. And Anita sees that Yolanda is like her: she can swim in the sea like it's home.

* * * * * * * *

The sea is reluctant to give them up. "Just a little longer," it seems to say. "Wait, I have something even more beautiful for you to share." In every corner is a new creature, a new revelation. Anita and Yolanda give themselves up to these temptations until Yolanda realizes they must go back. At long last, she guides the girl to land.

On the beach, Anita is too shy to say anything.

They walk up the shore, dripping water onto the sand as they head back to the seawall. They sit, and Yolanda says, "You see... you're not alone."

Anita bursts into tears. She's surprised to find herself crying. She hasn't felt lonely... she has too many friends in the sea to be lonely. But she has felt... not... normal.

Yolanda reaches for her hand, holding it gently. In her soothing voice, she repeats, "You're not alone... and it's not just me."

Anita turns to her, her blurry eyes searching Yolanda's face.

Yolanda continues, "When I was a girl, there were not many of us. But these are dangerous times, Tita. The Earth is hurting. It is sick..."

Anita listens. The Earth sick? Hard to believe, and yet... she remembers the pale coral... the litter on the beaches... the disappearing vaquitas...

"But the Earth has many defenses. One of them is us."

"Us?"

"The Sisterhood."

Anita hears the word, and something ancient in her stirs.

"The Sisterhood is growing every day, Tita. Mother Earth is making more of us than ever before... It is my role to train the new sisters... Next month, we're holding a training camp in Costa Rica. I want you to come. I want you to come and learn the ways of The Sisterhood."

"Costa Rica?" Anita has never left Mexico. There's no way her family could afford it.

"The Sisterhood will pay for it, Tita."

"What about the vaquitas? I can't just leave them."

"The vaquitas are in mortal trouble, Tita. The last five years, I've been trying to save them... but my efforts haven't worked. And now there are very few left."

Not wanting to hear anymore, Anita wishes she could shut her ears as Yolanda continues, "I'm not sure they can make it. We think there are thirty left. It may not be enough to breed."

21

Anita thinks of her new friend Esperanza and her eyes fill with tears. It seems so cruel to have picked the name "Hope" for her — just last night — and to be hearing this now.

"I know you want to protect the vaquitas, Tita. But I'm not sure it's the best use of your gift. It may be too late."

"No! NO!" Anita shakes off Yolanda's hand and stands up. Fiercely, she yells into Yolanda's face, "It is not too late!"

Yolanda stands up and embraces her. The girl sobs against her shoulder. For a long time Anita sobs, and in that crying is love for every creature that leaves this world.

Finally, her tears are spent. She becomes quiet, and the two sit back down together.

"Come to the training camp, Tita. And then you can return here, and protect the vaquitas if you choose. Or join another mission."

Anita doesn't say anything. She's mulling over everything Yolanda has told her.

"Shall we meet here at midnight tomorrow? And you can tell me your answer?"

Suddenly galvanized, Anita stands up. "Make it 11:30." She can't waste a single moment. The vaquitas need her.

"11:30 it is." She gets up and hugs Anita, murmuring into the girl's ear, "Give those vaquitas my best."

Anita nods into Yolanda's shoulder. Then they separate. Yolanda leaves, and Anita returns to the sea.

* * * * * * * *

"I'm much later than last night! I hope they didn't give up on me!" Anita says with some desperation as she rockets through the water and back to the Coral Garden.

She comes across the little boy first. He's got a vine of seaweed hanging around his neck.

"Leo!" she cries, naming him on the spot. "That's quite a mane!" she hugs him and as she does so, Esperanza and the adult male come swimming in.

"Espy! Virgil!" she hugs them both, not even sure where

the name "Virgil" came from. It just felt right. "Yolanda Rios said to give you her best!"

The vaquitas click back. In recognition? Just as Anita wonders about that, Virgil speeds off.

Something in his manner reminds her of all her old swimming contests. She laughs, "Oh, a game of chase, hmm?" Then she races to catch up. Espy follows, then little Leo.

They play for hours. Anita finally tears herself away, instructing them, "Stay where we were tonight."

The three bow their heads, "We will."

Anita blasts through the water to the beach, racing against her parents' alarm.

* * * * * * * *

"I must be more careful!" she scolds herself as her heart beats double-time and her jelly legs barely drag her down the street. The town is waking up. Luckily, her house remains dark, even as lights go on in neighboring ones.

Anita slips inside and into her room. Pulling at the clinging suit, she finally manages to get it off. She throws on her nightshirt and collapses onto the bed. She falls asleep instantly.

* * * * * * * *

An hour later, the alarm wakes her. Her first thought is: "There's no way I can go to that camp."

She spends all day considering it. Taking orders, she imagines the girls she would meet. Making tortillas, she imagines Espy getting caught in a net while she's away. Washing dishes, she thinks about what Yolanda said: that the vaquitas might be beyond hope.

She feels a pull to go, partly for herself, but mostly to avoid disappointing Yolanda. But her mind always comes back to the original thought: there's no way she can go.

* * * * * * * *

In the darkness, Yolanda is waiting on the seawall.

"I can't go," Anita says in greeting. Best to get it out.

"I thought you'd decide that," Yolanda says kindly. She motions for Anita to sit beside her.

Settling in, Anita explains, "My mother needs me at the restaurant. Summer is our busiest time..."

Yolanda listens. Yes, that's part of it...

Anita's voice chokes up, "And I can't leave my vaquitas. Even if... it's too late for them... I want to be with them. Even if it's just to watch them go..."

Yolanda puts her arm around her. Then she says, "I've been thinking, too, Tita. I think Life wants you here. I think maybe, just maybe, you will turn it around for the vaquitas."

A spark of hope rises in Anita. She knows Yolanda would never say this just to make her feel better.

Yolanda reaches into a bag at her feet. "I brought you something. A gift from The Sisterhood." She takes out a box and hands it to her. "It's waterproof and has GPS. Wear it in health, and with our love."

Anita opens the case and lifts out the watch. Even with eyes unaccustomed to luxury, she can see that it was very expensive. She straps it onto her left wrist, then says, "You never explained how you knew my wrist hurt."

"Yes, I forgot!" laughs Yolanda. "Stand up and face me, Tita."

Anita gets up. Standing, she is barely taller than Yolanda sitting.

"Hold out your right arm." Yolanda presses her right wrist against Anita's. At first there is a burning sensation. Then, as if embers were being coaxed into a fire, an orange glow appears. Then the orange turns to green. Yolanda lifts her arm away, and a tiny image of a tree shines from each woman's skin.

"Your wrist will tell you many things, Tita. It will tell you when a sister is nearby. It will tell you when danger is near. And it will tell you: pay attention."

* * * * * * * *

24

The glow from their wrists fades and then disappears. Yolanda gets up to leave. "Tita, always remember you're not alone. If it gets to be too much... or if you need any help at all... our number is in the case."

Anita hugs the woman one last time, then she watches Yolanda leave the beach. In the dim light, the woman quickly vanishes.

Sighing, Anita prepares for her swim. From her bag, she takes out her flashlight and her knife, and straps each of these onto her thigh. She isn't sure why she still bothers with the knife, but maybe it will come in handy.

She puts the watchcase in her bag, and hides it all under a motor boat. Then she goes to her vaquitas.

* * * * * * * *

The trio is waiting for her in the Garden. Moved by their faith in her, Anita feels the rightness of her decision. Her place is by their side.

"Shall we go to La Roca?" Anita asks. She wants to enlarge the area they visit, and look for nets and other vaquitas. The Rock is a place she loved as a child; her father would take her in his boat to visit the sea lions.

The vaquitas don't understand, but happily follow Anita. They swim many miles and finally reach the islet, really just a high rock in the sea.

It's surprisingly quiet. Anita's daytime visits were always so noisy, the birds and sea lions shouting over each other. Breaking the silence, Anita asks, "Are there vaquitas here?"

"No," clicks Espy, looking at the cliff face with curiosity.

No other vaquitas, Anita sighs. But she tries to be positive: at least they didn't see any nets!

They make the long swim back to the Coral Garden. When Anita says goodbye, she tries to apologize for making them swim so far. But the porpoises just smile.

* * * * * * * *

Anita's muscles are exhausted by the time she finally makes it home and into bed.

She wakes a few hours later, with one overwhelming thought: "I need food!"

Thank heavens, her mother's at the restaurant, and her father's out. She walks to the refrigerator and grabs the leftovers of last night's dinner. She wolfs them down, then hurries off to work.

At the restaurant, Anita can't stop smiling. The vaquitas are adorable and she gets to swim with them!

She doesn't even mind when Sr. Jiménez teases her: "You're looking very well today, Tita. Pedro comes home soon. I know he'll be happy to see you!"

Sr. Jiménez always thinks she must be crazy about his son. Is he nuts? Pedro, who kicked sand in her face when she was little? "But who cares about him? Tonight I'll get to the Garden early! I can't wait to see Esperanza and the boys!"

* * * * * * * *

TONY BAI

Listen, folks, it's just business. If I didn't do it, someone else would.

The bladders are getting harder to get, which makes it all riskier. But the risk makes it all a little more exciting. Plus, when the bladders are hard to get, the money just gets bigger.

The town is depressing. Proud of its fishing heritage. Proud of being suckers, I'd say. Proud of stinking like dying shrimp. I'm glad I don't have to go down there too often.

I'm meeting the kid at the border tomorrow. Before him that idiot Oscar ran the goods for us. He had a Border Crossing Card and could drive them up. But Oscar got caught with twenty bladders – impounded by Customs. Since there were really forty bladders on that job, guess what? The Customs guy must've syphoned off twenty... probably retired then, huh?

Oscar didn't serve time but needless to say neither I nor my boss would welcome him back. In fact, I'm pretty sure Shar would take care of him once and for all if he could.

No one knows where Oscar is now. Lying low. You don't lose Shar's money and not pay. And make no mistake: it's Shar Ping's money. Even those fish swimming in the sea right now – they don't know it yet, but they're Shar Ping's.

Yep, so it's up to me. What else is new? Up to me to drive the merchandise up to L.A. or Long Beach. Hand over my nice blue U.S. passport and act cool. "Hello, Officer." "Yes, I live in San Diego. Born and raised." "'Anything to report, Mr. Bai?'" "No, Officer." "'Have a nice day.'" "You, too, Officer."

Then drive on through.

Forty bladders in the floorboards. A cool $8,000 for me, and fifty times that for Shar.

It's easy money.

* * * * * * * *

ESPY

The humanfish has named me Esperanza. She says I give her hope. But she is the one giving hope.

She calls my friends Leo and Virgil. We appreciate these names, and recognize them as signs of affection. Our names for each other are noises she cannot make.

I like the sound: "Ess-per-ran-za." It is quite ladylike, I think. I

27

wish my sister would come round so I could tell her. And so I could introduce her to the humanfish.

Virgil and I decided right away that we could trust the humanfish. I am not sure why this is, considering what the humans have done to us. Leo, of course, follows our lead, and is happy to welcome her. He is still a child, after all. But, having lost so much, he does not trust everyone. So if he trusts her, too, that is a good sign.

* * * * * * * *

Anita is swimming with the pod in complete darkness. Reluctantly, she reaches to her thigh and unclips the flashlight. It doesn't feel right to drown the sea with artificial light. But what choice does she have? She has to see to protect her flock.

She turns the light on and off, following the group as it makes its way. They stay in a loose diamond formation, with Esperanza in front, and Virgil and Leo to the sides. Anita brings up the rear.

She has the light on again and is sweeping it from side to side when she sees it: a mesh that shouldn't be there. Virgil is heading right into it.

Anita speeds up to overtake him, and blocks his body with hers. At first he thinks it's a game, and he moves around her. But Anita pushes on his side, then points as she shines the light directly on the net.

Now Virgil sees it. He swerves away.

"Good job, Virgil."

He gives a low click.

Anita finds saying goodbye that night especially hard. She worries about them every day, of course, but now she's reminded what they're up against.

"Those nets are almost invisible," she says angrily, walking home.

* * * * * * * *

ESPY

Tonight we learned what the swallowing device is. Just the memory of it fills me with dread. It makes me scared in my own sea. Those "netzz" have turned my home into a place of danger. Even the word buzzes with menace. Thank goodness Virgil did not enter it.

And thank goodness the humanfish has come to help us.

* * * * * * * *

Anita knows she can't keep this up. She's had night after night of swimming with the vaquitas, and day after day of working at the restaurant. She's surviving on two or three hours of sleep. And she's eating so much she worries she'll cut into their family income.

But how can she stop?

On last night's patrol, she found a frantic Esperanza – or had Espy found her? – who led her to a net trapping Leo.

The situation looked dire. The animal was still. Anita feared he was dead.

She got to work right away, finding the tension points and cutting at them with the bowie knife. Thank God it was a rope net instead of the dense plastic kind. One by one the net lines tore away, and at last Anita was able to free the boy. With arms and snouts, she and Espy and Virgil pushed him up to the surface.

Leo showed no sign of life. In desperation, Anita made a fist and whacked his back. She did this several times, and just when she was about to give up, small snuffling noises came from his blowhole. She pushed on his side, vaguely hoping she could squeeze him back to life. Virgil began pushing his other side.

The wheezing noises continued from the blowhole. Were they getting louder? Stronger? Or was that just wishful thinking? She caught Espy's eye and could see her wrestling with the same thoughts.

"God, please, please," Anita begged, as it became clear the young creature was struggling to catch his breath.

After what seemed like hours, Leo rolled over on his side, then rolled to his other side, then gave a tremendous eruption of his blowhole.

Laughing, crying, Anita exclaimed, "¡Salud! God bless you!"

* * * * * * *

Anita worries all day about Leo. Will he be ok? Her mother scolds her for being distracted, "You took the wrong food to that customer! Wake up!"

Apologizing, Anita thinks about telling her mother what's going on. Maybe if there's a quiet moment...

Sr. Jiménez arrives. "Pedro is coming home today," he announces, paternal pride on his face.

Anita wants to say, "Why are you proud of him? The sand-kicker? He's awful!" But she stays quiet and listens to María chat with him.

As they're talking, and Anita's mind goes back to Leo, a red Mazda races past on the malecón. Its brakes screech, and the driver reverses up the road, wheeling into a parking space near the restaurant.

Sr. Jiménez calls out for the entire restaurant to hear, "That's my Pedro!"

* * * * * * *

ESPY

Anita will not come until nighttime.

I know her name now: A-nee-tah. I can almost produce it with my clicks.

30

She will not come until nighttime. During the day, she helps other humans with their feeding. They cannot do it alone. I think they are not very smart.

Virgil tells me not to be scared, that where we swim today is safe. But we thought it was safe last night. And Leo was almost swallowed up.

I feel the netzz closing in.

Leo was very shaken. But now, he behaves like nothing happened. He and Virgil are in the shallows, competing to see who can eat more. I hope it is not an act. I do not want him feeling the horrible fear that I feel. A fear that has settled on my heart.

It is a terrible thing not feeling safe in one's home.

* * * * * * *

Pedro has joined his father in the restaurant. He stares at Anita as she approaches to take their lunch orders.

"You've grown up, Tita," he says wolfishly.

Sr. Jiménez argues, "She is barely 5'2" and a hundred pounds! That is hardly grown!"

"I'm 5'3!" she protests inwardly.

"Pedro was telling me about his fishing charters – he just led a trip out of Cabo San Lucas! Lots of rich Americans. They listen to what my Pedro tells them."

Anita thinks, "Since when did Pedro know the difference between a shrimp and a sailfish?" But she manages a weak smile. "Welcome home, Pedro," she says. "Are you staying a while?"

"Just a week. But maybe I should make it longer." Anita doesn't take his bait. She turns and goes back to the kitchen.

* * * * * * *

EL JEFE

Word has reached me that the small boy in the north almost died. A witness to it, a ray I know, describes a strange creature hitting him. The hitting was violent, and, yet, the boy survived. The witness even wonders if the hitting helped him survive.

Strange. I do not understand. My sister says she will go. She is overdue in visiting the young ones that dwell in the Garden. All their parents are gone. They need her company and guidance.

* * * * * * * *

Anita gets to the beach later than usual that night. Her parents took forever to go to bed. As she heads to the water, she sees several dark lumps lying on the sand. Each is about five feet long. She unstraps her flashlight and examines them. Five totoaba, slashed in the thorax. Blood darkens the sand.

"They took the bladders," she murmurs. How long ago were the poachers here?

Looking cautiously around, she sees no one on the shore, and hears nothing but the waves.

She feels relief when she enters the water. "I feel safe here." If only the same were true for the totoaba. And for her vaquitas.

She swims to the Garden. Though she's late, Espy is still waiting for her, and leads her to the boys. To Anita's utter delight, there's another vaquita with them. She's even bigger than Espy, and older. Anita names her Abuelita (Little Granny.)

At first, Anita doesn't think Abuelita likes her. The porpoise stares into her eyes, and then makes several clicks that sound like "Tsk Tsk Tsk." Anita just floats in the water under this inspection, and tries to radiate loving thoughts.

At long last, the examination is over. Anita holds her breath, awaiting the verdict.

The matriarch appears satisfied, because now she produces a series of clicks that sound like "Coo Coo Coo." Her heart swelling, Anita reaches out to pat Abuelita. But instead the old dear caresses Anita's wrist with her snout. To the wonderment of all, a golden glow starts to shine from her wrist. The warm light suffuses the group, and they all gaze at one another.

They spend a wonderful night together, Abuelita leading the pod. When Anita finally leaves, she recalls the gutted totoaba, and says: "Be especially careful! Stay where we swam together."

The porpoises click back to her, "We will."

* * * * * * * *

ABUELITA

Thank the Creator, help has come. When I arrived in the Garden today, the young ones told me what happened. They explained that what the ray had seen was true: a humanfish had helped our small dear one. Still, I worried their faith in her was misplaced, the dreams of youth. But tonight I met her for myself and instantly knew she was sent to help us.

My brother will be relieved. I know he feels guilty that he cannot patrol everywhere and has not been to the Garden in a long time.

The guilt is unfounded. He is old. He asks too much of himself.

I will swim to him tomorrow and tell him.

* * * * * * * *

Anita meets up with Espy and the boys the next night. "Where's Abuelita?" she wonders. "Where are all the others, for that matter?" But no answers come.

Leo interrupts her worries by nudging her, "Look over there." In the distance, dolphins are leaping into the star-filled sky.

"Shall we try it, Leo?" Anita giggles. He nods.

Side by side, they start to swim, slowly gathering speed. Then they try to jump out of the water... Oof. Each of them gets zero clearance above the surface.

Espy and Virgil sit in the water nearby, laughing at the efforts of their friends.

"I guess neither of us is made for this," Anita says. Leo clicks in sad agreement.

Virgil buzzes, "Let's go watch them." So the four swim over to the dolphins and give them an audience. Watching their beautiful acrobatics, Anita claps loudly, forgetting to be afraid that poachers might be in earshot.

After a happy night, she advises the porpoises, "Stay in this area tomorrow."

* * * * * * * *

EL JEFE

My sister says there is a human-shaped creature who is helping our tribe in the Garden. I am skeptical. I wonder what the creature wants.

And yet... was this the source of the joy I felt the other night?

I could swim north to meet her, but my place is here. I must concentrate my efforts where most of my brethren live.

The young ones have told us of the netzz. So now I know what I am looking for. I knew the humans were diabolical but now I understand the form it takes. I wonder what they want from us?

These questions hurt my head, and I must rest.

If I were not so tired, I would celebrate: no deaths today. Thirty-six of us will greet the new sun.

* * * * * * *

Though Anita is permanently exhausted, she feels quite energetic the next day and thinks she's back to doing a good job waiting tables. So she's somewhat surprised when María tells her that she wants to talk to her.

"Yes, Mamá?"

"Tita, you know your father and I love you."

"Yes..." Anita looks at her mother and realizes how nervous María is.

"We are here for you no matter what."

Anita says nothing. She's waiting for the punchline.

"I haven't said anything to your father, because we know what a temper he can have."

Still waiting.

"Are you in trouble?"

Anita almost blurts out, "I'm not in trouble, but I'm so worried about Espy and..." and then she realizes what her mother is talking about.

María: "You're eating twice as much as before, Tita. And we know you go out sometimes at night... Are you pregnant?"

Anita doesn't know whether to laugh or cry. She finds herself laughing out loud, and saying, "No, Mamá. I'm not pregnant." And then tears come, "But I haven't been honest with you."

* * * * * * *

MARÍA

I don't feel right lying to Miguel, but what choice do I have? Until I know what is going on with our daughter, I can't worry him.

Is she mentally ill? That is the only explanation. I know she would never lie to me.

Swimming like a fish? A secret society? Protecting the vaquita? My sixteen year old daughter?

We've told her father we are going to the neighbor's.

But we're heading to the beach. Tita says she will show me everything.

* * * * * * * *

It's a lovely summer evening, and people are milling outside on the beach. Anita tells her mother they should walk farther along, to a bend in the shore where they won't be seen.

María, struggling in confusion and worry, just follows her daughter's directions.

Anita tells her to sit on the sand. "Keep an eye on me and on the watch." The watch is new to María, and obviously very costly, something the Pérez family could never afford.

Anita walks straight into the sea. She doesn't even swim, just walks until the waves overtake her.

Her mother stares at the watch. What's the longest someone can hold her breath? María grew up in Baja and remembers the contests of her childhood. What had been her best? Two minutes?

Two minutes go by, then three. María starts to worry. Is her daughter ok?

Four minutes go by. María starts to panic. She's just about to run in when she sees her daughter's raised thumb: "I'm ok." Six minutes, seven, eight. Finally, after twelve minutes, Anita emerges, showing no sign of exertion.

María is speechless as her daughter returns. Anita hugs her as if to say, "It's really me."

* * * * * * * *

MARÍA

I can't believe it. Could you? And yet I feel a strange calm, that all is as it should be.

I've cried many times about those poor vaquitas. And now my daughter is protecting them.

I tell her how proud I am. And ask her to promise me she will be careful.

* * * * * * * *

Anita promises she'll be careful. Then she asks, "Do you think we should tell Papá?"

"No," María says adamantly. "There are dangerous things going on. He would just worry."

Anita knows the secrecy will be a burden. She reaches out to hug her mother... and her wrist starts to hurt. Soon it starts to shine with yellow light, as bright as an incandescent lightbulb. Anita looks to the water. "I think they are nearby, Mamá..."

She runs down and dives into the water, swimming just beyond the break. There, where they've never been, are Espy, Virgil, and Leo. "I don't know how you knew... but thank you," Anita says to them. Then they all surface together.

"They're here to honor you," she calls to her mother.

And María sees what no one in the world has ever seen: three live vaquitas, right near the shoreline. And they're bowing their heads to her.

In a day of surprises, María isn't sure, but this might top them all. She stands on the sand and bows back to them.

Anita calls to her, "I must take them back to the Refuge. It was dangerous for them to come here." Even though vaquitas aren't hunted, Anita doesn't want them near humans.

María nods to her, tells her to be safe, and heads home. As she walks, she knows that her daughter is no longer a child.

And she realizes Anita will never leave their town. For this, she is both grateful and sad.

* * * * * * * *

The next day, a new energy fills the restaurant. Anita and María have always worked well together, but now they're truly partners. Anita feels relieved not having to lie to her anymore.

She tells her, "I've been thinking... I feel sure we could ask The Sisterhood for a small income, to help with the food I'm eating."

María laughs. "We're not poor yet, Tita! We can manage it. I was just worried you were eating for two."

"I'm eating for four," she laughs. "Or five, if Abuelita's around."

* * * * * * * *

Anita's swim that night is uneventful. She catches up with Espy, Virgil, and Leo at the Coral Garden; Abuelita joins them later. They don't see any nets. As always, she tells them to stay in the areas they've been in that night.

As she's swimming back to shore, inexplicably, she decides to surface early. Usually she surfaces only near the end. But tonight she comes up four hundred feet from the beach. Above the water, she takes a moment to enjoy the moon, which is almost full. Childlike, she's just about to howl like a wolf, when she stops herself.

She turns her head to listen more keenly. The night is completely silent.

Just as she's about to dive under and make the final push for the beach, she hears something. A tiny buzzing noise. She cocks her ear to the source and strains to hear more. It gets much louder, and she realizes it's a boat coming fast.

Instinctively, she dives deep. "It's probably just people out having fun," she tells herself, somehow feeling that isn't true. Nervously, her fingers play with the sand of the sea floor.

She stays underwater long enough for the boat to land. Then she surfaces and slowly approaches the beach. She can see there are three men unloading the panga, the small fishing boat. But she can't make out any details. A white buoy rests between her and the shore.

"I can swim to that to get a closer look," she thinks, then dips back under without a sound.

Luckily the distance is short, because there are no landmarks (or watermarks) to guide her. She stays ten feet under, looking for the white plastic bottom of the buoy above her. When she sees it, she stops and swims up to meet it, and puts her arms around it.

Clinging to the base of the buoy, she slowly lifts her head to peep out. She sees two figures hoisting big fish out of the boat, which has a dark hull ("bad guys in black," she notes.) A third man is slashing at the bodies, then plunging his hand into their carcasses to rip something out. He throws these parts into a pail.

"Hurry up!" says one of the men. "We have to get moving!"

Scared but determined to get a better look, Anita decides to leave the safety of the buoy. She slips beneath the water and swims a few more feet. Rising above the surface again, she's close enough to see that all three men are young. The one with the knife has a strong build. His white T-shirt glows in the moonlight, stretched over the muscles of his arms and chest.

Peering at him, trying to discern his features, she hears him cry, "What the...?" Staring at his feet, he growls, "This is one of those dumb porpoises."

"Leave it, let's get out of here!" The other two turn the boat and start dragging it down the sand.

The man with the knife grabs the pail and runs to the water, jumping in the boat after them.

Anita steals a moment to get a good look at the three. But they're a blur of movement, and she knows they're coming her way. Fearing for herself, and knowing she has to get to that vaquita, she dives deep.

The wake shakes her as the boat speeds past, back out to sea, to find harbor farther down the coast.

* * * * * * * *

Anita has swum fast many times. Fast, in races as a child. How silly they seem now. Fast, to get home before her parents wake up. Even that seems silly. This time, she swims as if every life in the world depends on it. "Maybe it's ok," she tells herself. "Maybe it wasn't in the net very long. It's on the beach – that's good, right? It can breathe on the beach!"

But even as she races, she knows the odds are slim. The men probably had those nets deployed all night. The vaquita likely died hours ago.

Hurtling in, she scrapes her legs and rips her wetsuit as she comes onto the beach. Her eyes dart across the pile of bodies, spotting the lump that is the vaquita. Please don't let it be Espy. Or Virgil, or Leo, or Abuelita.

Please be alive, please, she says as she frantically pushes the dead totoaba bodies out of the way, freeing the vaquita's body.

It's not one of her friends, she can tell that right away. She shakes its body. There's no movement. She shakes it again, violently. Nothing.

She whacks its back, like she did that day with Leo. Nothing, nothing, nothing. The black button eyes are frozen.

She slumps to the sand, sobbing. She has failed this one.

* * * * * * * *

Anita sits watch by the dead vaquita. Exhausted by the long night, and by all the crying, she's in a daze. Eventually she realizes dawn has come. In the pink light, she stands up and notices little seashells scattered nearby. She gathers some and places the shells around the body, making a memorial.

She wishes her mother were here. She wants to call her but can't. It's not just being in a wetsuit; Anita is probably the only teenager in town without a cellphone.

She doesn't know what to do.

"I can't just leave it here!"

She considers pushing the animal into the water to return it home. But she rejects that idea. Maybe there's something to learn from it that would help the others. So she decides to keep vigil until someone comes along and she can ask for help.

She checks her watch: 6:30. Her parents will be up soon. How long before they notice she's not there?

Anita is singing softly to the dead vaquita when she sees something move. She looks up, and there is Coco, running down the beach towards her.

"Coco, how did you know?" she cries, petting him, and murmuring, "Good, good boy" into his fur.

Then she stands up and says, "You must protect this, Coco," gesturing to the hulk that was the vaquita. Coco sniffs at it and lets out a low whine. "I have to go home to get help. Stand by it and don't let anyone interfere." At the head of the porpoise, Coco sits on his haunches, every inch the sentry, looking down the beach.

* * * * * * * *

Anita races home. She opens the door and can hear her father singing in the shower.

Her mother exclaims, "Tita, I was worried about you. And now Coco is gone!"

"Coco is helping me, Mamá." In a rush of words, she explains the situation.

María suggests they call the marine mammal sanctuary.

"But they won't open for hours!" Anita cries.

"Tita, I can handle the restaurant. You go to the beach and keep watch with Coco. I will keep calling the marine center until I reach someone."

* * * * * * * *

41

COCO

I could feel Tita was in need. The air became very heavy. I was visiting my mother's spot and her spirit told me, "Go, Coco! Go to Tita at the beach!"

Now I am here on the sand near the sea creature. I have seen these creatures before. They love to play. Once I played with one. That was a happy day. But lately I have not seen them.

This one will not play in our sea anymore. I can tell it is dead. Maybe it will meet my mother.

These boys do not seem naughty. But I am not sure, so I bark. I will make sure they do not touch the sea creature.

* * * * * * * *

Anita heads back to the beach. Even far away, she can see Coco's doing an excellent job protecting the vaquita. Two pre-teen boys are cowering about twenty feet away, and Coco's barks can be heard all the way down the malecón.

As Anita approaches she says, "Hey, boy, it's me," and Coco stops barking. The two boys look afraid and one starts to run off. The other one, who's a little older, says, "We weren't doing anything wrong."

Anita looks at him. He's a local boy she's seen many times on the malecón, skateboarding or kicking a soccer ball with his friends. She always thought his face seemed kind. "It's ok," she says. "Coco is protecting the vaquita because I told him to."

"That's what we were wondering! It *is* a vaquita, isn't it?!"

"Yes, I'm afraid it is."

They draw a little closer and Anita gestures them closer still. "Not many people get to see a vaquita," she says. "They belong to our town. We have to protect them. We let this one down."

The boys are acting tough, but Anita spies a few tears.

"What will happen now?" asks the older one.

"I'm waiting for staff from the sanctuary. We called them this morning when I found it."

"We'll wait, too."

Anita doesn't argue. School's not in session, and even if it were, this is a good lesson for them. "I'm Anita," she offers.

"I'm Juan Carlos, and this is Antonio. Your mother owns the restaurant, right?"

"Yes." Gesturing towards the body, she asks, "Do you know about vaquitas?"

Juan Carlos nods. "My mother says they're magical. She saw one when she was nineteen... the next day, my father proposed."

Antonio adds, "My father doesn't think they exist anymore. He says it wasn't the fishing that caused the problem, but the Americans changing the Colorado River."

Anita says, "It's true that there's very little fresh water coming into our sea anymore. I'm not sure that affected the vaquita, but the totoaba aren't breeding like they once did. The salt level isn't right."

"I heard that totoaba is worth more than gold," says Juan Carlos.

"No way!" Antonio replies. "A fish?!"

Anita talks with the boys for about an hour, and it does her good. They're sweet-natured and they're interested in what she tells them about the vaquitas. It feels good to know someone's interested, even if it's just young kids.

After they talk for a while, the boys fan out to gather more shells. They come back with handfuls, adding to the burial tribute.

A young man and a middle-aged woman walk down the beach and Anita sees that they're wearing uniforms of the marine sanctuary. The woman wears a camera around her neck and the man has a tarp dangling over his shoulder.

Anita feels a sense of ownership as they begin taking photos and asking her what she knows. She points out the dead totoaba and they take photos of them, too. They're polite but don't seem to care like she does. Will they do right by the body? She wants to ask but fears the answer.

After they finish taking photos and jotting notes down, the man lays the tarp on the ground and begins to push the vaquita onto it. Without being asked, Anita helps him, touching the animal's smooth skin. It's much colder than when she first found it. She asks, "Can you tell if it's a boy or a girl?"

The woman answers, "It's a female – a young adult." At this the woman shows her first sign of emotion: sighing, she says, "A great loss. There aren't that many of child-bearing age left."

Juan Carlos and Antonio offer to help carry the animal to the truck but the man kindly tells them they can manage. He and the woman thread ropes through the end of the tarp. On the count of three, they lift the carcass, and between them, they carry it down the beach.

Anita watches them go. Her new friends take some of the shells and hand them to her. Juan Carlos says, "Don't cry. It will be ok."

But Anita doesn't think it will be.

* * * * * * * *

COCO

Those boys have gone. They were good boys. Now it is just my Tita and me on the beach.

Tita is so sad. She is sad the way I was when my mother died.

I sit with her on the sand. Finally she gets up and says, "Come on, Coco. Time for you to go home and for me to go help Mamá at the restaurant." One of her paws is full of the rocks the boys gave her.

We walk down to the street. When we get to the house with spiky plants, I know that is where I turn to go home. But

44

instead I stay by her side. She stops and gently pushes me, and so I go home to our yard. Tita keeps walking, the little rocks still in her paw.

* * * * * * *

Anita has the handful of shells in her fist when she arrives at the restaurant. It's late for breakfast but the restaurant is busier than it's been for a while. She carefully puts the shells on a shelf, then dives in to helping her mother. The activity helps take her mind off the girl. But it doesn't work entirely. She keeps seeing her little gray body shining on the beach.

"I'll call her Lola."

Sadness comes in a wave as she realizes she'll never swim with her. "Rest in peace, little Lola."

During a slow part of lunch, Anita tells her mother about the morning, and about the boys she met.

She toys with the shell pile and chooses a particularly pretty one. "I'll make this into a necklace," she says, "in honor of Lola and the vaquitas."

* * * * * * *

That night, it's with a heavy heart that Anita approaches the Coral Garden. Will her friends know? In her time with them, she's discovered they seem to communicate with many creatures in the sea.

If they haven't heard, should she tell them? She thinks she should keep it a secret. They don't need more bad news.

She's waiting at the Garden when Virgil comes up to her, then Leo. That's unusual – Espy always comes to her first. Panic sets in for Anita. Has something happened to Espy?

She flashes her eyes at the boys but the water is dim and they can't see her expression. Besides, they've never been as good at reading her thoughts as Espy. All she can do is follow them.

The boys lead her to a shallow area. Espy is there, hanging

in the water, barely moving. Anita sees her take an occasional breath, so she's ok physically. But something is wrong.

The water is so low that Anita stands, level with Espy at the surface. Face to face, she looks at the porpoise intently. "Espy?"

The animal doesn't reply.

"You know about her, don't you?"

Low clicks come from behind, as Virgil answers for her.

Anita just stands and waits. And then she knows. She can't say how, but she knows.

"She was your sister, wasn't she?"

Espy looks at her. And for the rest of her life, Anita will swear there were tears in Espy's eyes.

* * * * * * * *

It's a solemn affair with her friends that night. They stay in the shallows and barely move. The boys eat a bit but Espy takes nothing.

Anita just stands in the shallows, a witness to their sadness.

Swimming back to the beach, she passes a gillnet. She is sure it wasn't there when she headed out, and that was definitely the route she took.

She'll worry all night now, because her vaquitas don't know the net has been put up.

"I'm not sure I can do this alone," she thinks.

* * * * * * * *

ELJEFE

The news from the north is not good: a young would-be mother is dead. Stolen from our sea, stolen from us, taken in the netzz.

Her sister is distraught. I would go to her but I have nothing to offer her. My sister will go and comfort her as best she can.

To think I had been feeling hopeful. What foolish weakness.

The truth must be faced: the humans want our extinction. I cannot fathom why.

I have spoken with a totoaba elder and their grief exceeds our own. Thank the Creator they cannot see what I have heard: that their bodies end up breathless on the sand, mutilated.

What will satisfy the human bloodlust? If giving myself would do so, I would.

Only thirty-five of us are left.

I begin to think I must swim out to meet the humanfish. If she cannot stop our destruction, perhaps she can record our history.

If she could tell our story, that would be something. Though we may die out, and never live again among the corals here, never swim again in the moonlight... at least the world would know of us.

But maybe it is the ego... the folly... of an old porpoise. Our Creator will always know and love us. So I must believe.

* * * * * * *

María tries her best to cheer Anita up over the next few days. Anita tries to pretend it's helping, but inside she feels lost.

She continues her nightly rounds, meeting up with the vaquitas in the Garden. Espy is slowly coming around, swimming more energetically. In this task, she seems to be prodded by Abuelita, who's now with the pod every night. "Abuelita is nudging Espy just like Mamá is nudging me..."

The net from several nights ago is gone; while that's good, she still worries that she's not covering enough of the Refuge.

"There are supposedly another thirty of you guys," she says to them. "When, or how, can I meet them?" But their button eyes just look blank.

* * * * * * * *

Anita gets a clue to the whereabouts of more vaquitas from a sad occurrence: another one is found dead, a young male this time, trapped in a gillnet in the far southern end of the Refuge. A place she hasn't visited much.

She overhears the news from customers at the restaurant. She escapes to the bathroom and sobs.

* * * * * * * *

MARÍA

Tita thinks she can fool me, but I know she's been crying.

Another dead vaquita. It's too much.

It's too much to ask of her. Just what is this "Sisterhood" exactly? And what right do they have to put this burden on a young girl?

* * * * * * * *

EL JEFE

I am becoming an old, old porpoise.

I feel bent in body and mind.

Can this really be happening to my tribe?

We just had the bad news out of the north: the death of the young could-have-been-mother.

And now, closer to home, here in my waters, we hear that young Odi is gone.

Thirty-four remain.

So much death in such a short time.

My patrols have done nothing. For all my experience, for all my so-called leadership, I am a failure.

Was it my arrogance? To take on the title of "Chief"? I humbly apologize to the Sea and Sun Creator. At this point all I ask is that You take us all into the Great Ocean, far away from humans. Let no humans enter that sacred water, and let our spirits swim there safely for eternity.

I want nothing to do with the humanfish. Since hearing of her, the deaths have increased. I do not think she means us well.

* * * * * * * *

Anita spends most of the day in a fog. But slowly her mind clears, and she comes to a conclusion: she must go south in search of vaquitas.

That evening, María waits up with her daughter for her husband to go to bed. As Anita's about to leave, her mother says, "Tita, tell me what you're thinking."

Her resolve weakens and she falls into a chair. The latest death has shaken her. "Mamá, I don't know what to say. Some days, I think it's helping – if nothing else, I'm protecting Espy and Leo and Virgil..."

María nods, urging her to continue.

"But then we get news like this, and I think: why do I care, and other people don't?"

"Sweetie, people DO care. A lot of people are asking for stronger poaching laws. And some of the fishermen have formed patrols. Your father is thinking about joining."

"Yes, you're right. That's true. But... is it enough? I don't know. I don't know what the magic number is. How low a number before they can't sustain a population?"

The whole village wonders this. When is it too late? Twenty? Ten? Or is it already too late?

"Tita, I have to tell you, I'm not happy with that society choosing you for this. You're just a young woman, still a girl."

Anita protests, "No, Mamá, you don't understand. They didn't choose me. Life chose me. This is what I'm supposed to do."

María knows Anita is right. Softening, she says, "Well, I think it's time you contacted them. Maybe they can send some help."

Anita hears her. But does she listen? She gets up and says, "I will when I need them, Mamá. I promise. And now I must go."

* * * * * * *

She swims to the Garden and says a quick hello to her four friends. Abuelita seems agitated, like she wants to tell her something. But Anita's in a hurry and blasts off to the south.

She's been to this section, but only a few times, and that was before she met any vaquitas. And lately? Well, she has to admit that she's been enjoying her quartet so much that she slacked off looking for others. But Lola's death and the southern boy's death have pushed her. She has to find the rest and she has to come up with a plan.

Swimming south, she notices how different it looks and feels from her northern sea. There's more coral and many more types of fish. It's also much deeper and at times she realizes she's going a bit too deep – she feels a tingling in her feet and hands. A sure sign she's heading too low.

She swims with great speed and intensity. "I have to cover more territory... I must find them!"

Her eyes try to focus on the sights in the water. Are there nets? Vaquitas? It's a full moon, but clouds cover it. No

50

glowing fish come in to help. "I can't see anything!" Anita cries in frustration.

As if hearing her, the night responds by putting her in a field of bioluminescent plankton. It's a shimmering field of turquoise. It's gorgeous, and seems to have no end.

But Anita can't play the tourist tonight. She's just thankful that the electric glow helps her look for nets.

Eyes down, searching, she's swimming at the surface. She raises her head to get her bearings and notices that the blue neon field is splitting in two. "What's happening?"

Then she understands: a dark mass is rising under the field, pushing the glow apart. "Mateo!" she cries, swimming to greet him. "I've missed you!"

He clicks back that he's missed her, too. Then he offers, "Can I give you a ride?"

A smile spreads over her face. "That would be great! To the south, please!"

With twice the speed that she could do, Mateo delivers her into the waters of the southern Refuge. Then he says goodbye and swims away.

Her happiness soon fades into disappointment. She finds no vaquitas that night. And it's a long swim back home.

* * * * * * * *

ABUELITA

Anita swam off so quickly I did not have time to react. I needed to stay with Esperanza, who is still grieving. But it would be best if I introduce Anita to my brother. Or at least alert him she is coming.

I will swim south now. Virgil promises to look after Esperanza.

* * * * * * * *

The next night, Anita is at it again. Swimming south, looking for more of her flock. There's plenty of moonlight, but still she's straining her eyes more than usual, desperate to find any rogue nets before they find any unsuspecting vaquitas.

Spotting the hulk of an old fishing boat below her, she thinks, "That can be my marker for the start of the southern Refuge." She notes its location with her GPS, then swims farther along.

She encounters a few totoaba, and gives them a smile. She feels guilty, though, because she hasn't been helping them.

"There's only so much you can do, Tita," she starts to say, when she sees it: a vaquita about the same size as Virgil.

Out of nowhere, she finds herself making a clicking noise like Espy always does in greeting. The animal stops and turns, inching slowly her way.

"I'm your friend, I'm your friend," Anita thinks and clicks. Her wrist starts to glow and the animal comes in to look.

"Hello," she says, as he stares at her wrist. "Can we swim together?"

The vaquita buzzes yes, excited by this strange creature.

Thrilled, Anita follows him, and for hours, they swim, exploring canyons she has never seen before.

When they finally part, Anita asks, "May I call you El Sud (the southern one)?"

The vaquita lowers his snout to nod.

"I am here to keep you safe. I'll come back tomorrow."

El Sud exhales from his blowhole: "See you tomorrow."

* * * * * * * *

EL JEFE

My sister tells me the humanfish has come to our southern waters. I have not seen her – but truthfully, I have not looked very hard. I do not want to meet her. My sister says I must.

The rays and turtles help me in my patrols. They check in with my brethren and report back to me. There is so much sea to cover and my eyesight worsens. And I cannot go into the Area.

There are still thirty-four of us, thank the Creator.

Will there ever again be thirty-five?

I will think about meeting the humanfish.

* * * * * * * *

Anita sees El Sud the next two nights. She loves her time with him, but she's frustrated she doesn't meet any others. And she's exhausted from covering so much territory.

A busy day at the restaurant worsens her fatigue. When the day is finally over, she puts away the last dishes and sighs, "And tonight I have to lie to Papá again."

As she heads home, she predicts another night of wasted effort. "I'll never find more vaquitas."

Feeling hopeless, she thinks about what her mother said, about calling The Sisterhood. Deep inside, she knows why she doesn't call. She's proud of her shepherding. And she's afraid that if she asks for help, the vaquitas will be taken away from her. They're her special project, aren't they?

Slowly it dawns on her she's being ridiculous. "They *will* be taken from me if they aren't saved."

She resolves to contact The Sisterhood in the morning.

* * * * * * * *

EL SUD

With his sister's help, I've convinced our chief to meet the humanfish. I will take him to her tonight.

I feel the tide is turning for us.

There's work to be done, but when it's over, I will find a vaqui girl. We will have children and they will live.

* * * * * * * *

TONY BAI

The kid tells me the fishermen aren't seeing totoaba much anymore. Looks like it's drying up. I gotta start thinking about my next move. Yep, if the totoaba business is dying, I gotta figure out what to do next. And how to convince Shar to go with it.

Don't get me wrong, it does make me kind of sad. End of a species and all that.

Actually, I gotta be honest: I couldn't care less.

Nature is borinnnngggggg. Give me technology any day. More than that, though, I like money. Money lets me have control.

I don't want anyone lording over me. I don't want someone ordering me around, telling me what to do. And God knows I don't want my parents' life, slaving away in a tiny restaurant. I still cringe when I think of customers complimenting their cooking. Oh, the condescension. I was always so embarrassed for them, and for me.

Sure, I have a boss, but he's seven thousand miles away. And he gives me autonomy. He gives me – what's that expression? He gives me "Enough rope to hang myself." Ha, I like that. Yeah, that's about it. I gotta be careful I don't hang myself.

But you gotta be willing to look death in the face. By working for Shar, that's what I do every day.

He'll be gone some day – naturally or not so naturally – and I'll be a rich man. From the work I've done for him. But also, who knows? Maybe he'll put me in his will. They say he doesn't have any kids.

That's a little fantasy I have. Tony Bai, heir to the Shar Ping fortune... and new chair of the Shar Ping Syndicate. You gotta dream. And keep your head down and your eyes and ears open.

If it all sounds a little like *The Godfather*, you're right. That movie's a favorite of mine.

* * * * * * * *

Anita's pessimistic mood pervades her swim. And now even her vaquita friends don't want her around. Espy and the boys and Abuelita don't seem sad to see her go.

"Are they mad at me?" she wonders. She feels they're pushing her away.

"Espy, are you ok?" she asks.

Espy touches her snout to Anita's forehead, giving her a gentle kiss. This is new, and reassuring... and is there something about the water? It seems to say, "Be off! The south awaits!"

Anita follows the sea's command and rushes to the southern section.

Before she even gets to the boat landmark, El Sud is upon her, his snout firmly touching her leg. She stops swimming and looks at him. The moon is bright, there are glowing plankton nearby, and a school of phosphorescent fish has stopped at her side. Then her wrist starts to glow. All is light itself for her. And there, beside Sud, is the largest vaquita she's ever seen.

The new animal takes no interest in her glowing wrist, but rather stares into her eyes, as if he's measuring her up. Anita gets the sense that he's seen a lot in his time. "You don't like humans, do you?"

El Jefe continues staring at her. After a full five minutes he turns to swim away. Anita is crushed. It hurts that he doesn't like or trust her.

But then she sees him stop and turn his head to her, as if to say, "Are you coming or aren't you?"

* * * * * * * *

Anita's heart soars, and a gigantic smile comes to her face as she hurries to catch up.

El Jefe and El Sud take her into a reef she's never seen before. It's like a miracle: every five minutes, they come across another vaquita. Some nibbling around the corals, some digging at the seabed. All lift their heads and take a moment to look at her. At each one, El Jefe makes some clicks.

After Anita has met twelve vaquitas, and her heart is swelling with elation ("This is where they are! THIS is where they are!") and thinking it can't get any better, El Jefe makes a piercing noise, unlike anything Anita has ever heard. It's like a scream. Anita becomes frightened but then sees twenty vaquitas gathered in a circle around her.

El Jefe clicks to introduce her. Anita says to the group: "I am so happy meeting you all."

Clicks.

"First, I want to say how sorry I am about what we humans have done to you."

More clicks, especially loud from El Jefe.

"We're not always skillful. We do things for dumb reasons, like money."

Silence. Clearly the vaquitas have no concept of this.

Anita reconsiders, then says, "We're hurt and scared and so we do things to try to make up for that. But many of us love you and are trying to protect you."

More clicks.

"I can help protect you. You know about the nets?"

A porpoise about the size of Espy is coaxed forward. There's a gravity and sadness about her, and Anita immediately knows she's the mother of the boy that was recently killed. The mother nods her head.

"I'll swim with you, and keep you from the nets!" Anita tells them. "Let her son be the last one killed!"

The vaquitas erupt into a chorus of excited clicks.

* * * * * * * *

EL JEFE

There can be no doubt the Creator has sent the humanfish to us. What hope she brings. There is a new energy and resolve among my tribe.

I almost wonder: is this my daughter, come back in a new form? How alike they are: petite, lithe, strong. A graceful swimmer with dark brown eyes.

The delusions of an old porpoise.

But I will make her my human daughter. She will protect us, and I will protect her.

* * * * * * * *

"Mamá, I can't begin to describe it. Last night in the South, I saw twenty-one vaquitas! Including their chief!"

Her mother listens, doubt overshadowing her happiness for her daughter. "That's wonderful, Tita. But I still don't think you can do it on your own. You need to call The Sisterhood."

"But I'm not doing it on my own! El Jefe and El Sud and Abuelita will help me... even Espy will help."

María listens but does not respond. She turns away and says, "It's time to prepare for lunch."

* * * * * * * *

That night, Anita finds it in their shed: an old rope net.

"Sorry, Papá," she says as she cuts out a section and ties it around her waist.

More like a fugitive than ever, she scurries down her dark street to the beach. She dives into the sea, feeling sad she can't see Espy. Her work lies south.

When she finds El Jefe, she asks him to herd the vaquitas together like he did last night. He calls out and slowly they come in. She can feel their reluctance. The crowd makes them nervous.

Anita addresses them: "I have a plan to help you, since I can't swim with each of you." The water is silent, the creatures waiting. "I've brought something with me."

Anita unwinds the rope belt. The fluorescing fish have all left, so she turns on her flashlight. Slowly she passes each member of the circle, shining light on the material in front of their snouts.

A few vaquitas wonder: is it seaweed?

Anita explains, "It's a portion of a gillnet."

The porpoises respond with agitated clicks, many backing away from the evil thing.

"I want to learn which of you has the best eyesight. And – for those who do – ask if you'd be willing to help the others."

The clicks subside as they ponder this. They wait for her to say more.

"I will attach this small piece to those two rocks... and then I'll ask you each to approach. When you see the net, make a noise and let me know. When you see it, ok? Not just because you know I put it there.

"Now let's break up a bit, to allow some of the glowing fishes back. It should be a normal evening in our sea – the usual conditions."

El Jefe disperses the herd, instructing them to divide into small groups and wait to be tested.

He goes first. Like the others, he knows exactly where the net is. Those two stones are as familiar to him as his own tail. Didn't he play chase among them with his brother? But his brother is long dead and his memory is no help. El Jefe's face is in the net before he sees it.

His manner noble, his pride unbowed, he goes to Anita's side to test the others.

In the dark murky water, with few glowing fish returning to help, one by one the vaquitas fare badly. A few can see the net at one foot. But most only see it at four or five inches. And a few get their snouts right into it.

Anita's heart is breaking. She feels the danger facing the creatures, and she also feels she's embarrassing them. She's about to call it off when two of the younger porpoises appear.

With youthful confidence, the one clicks to the other. Anita senses he's boasting he can do better than his friend. The other argues back.

The slighter youngster, with white spots on its fin, goes first. With a dramatic flair, he swims back ten feet. He comes swimming in fast, and at the five foot mark, he clicks, "I see it."

Anita gets excited... but is he just showing off? To test him again, she says, "This is one finger" – she holds up one finger – "and this is two fingers" – she holds up two fingers. "Do you understand?"

One finger, she gestures. Click, he replies.

Two fingers, she gestures. Click click, he replies.

"Great!" Anita says, "Stay there." She swims five feet from him and stops.

Looking at him, her hopes fade. In the dim light, her own sharp eyes can only pick out the markings on his fin. "Please work," she murmurs. Slowly, almost in defeat, she raises two fingers.

He clicks twice.

Relief runs through her and she cries, "Ok, Spots, good job!"

By now, the other youngster is itching to go. He backs up fifteen feet, comes swimming in, and clicks at ten feet from the net.

"Vente/Vente (20/20) – that's what I'll call you!"

Anita confirms Vente's extraordinary vision with several

more tests. She's very pleased; now all she has to do is make sure they're willing to help.

"El Jefe, can we talk to these two? They might listen to you better than to me."

All the other vaquitas have slowly left. While it was exciting – the humanfish is very pretty, such an interesting creature – her face has two blowholes instead of one! – well, it was too crowded.

With the bulk of El Jefe providing the gravitas the situation requires, Anita tells the young porpoises, "Did you understand me last night? When I said it's dangerous for vaquitas?"

Yes clicks.

"I want you to have long lives. And I want your families to have long lives."

Slightly bored clicks. They're young and feeling slightly hungry. Can they go now?

Appeal to their male pride, she thinks.

"I need your help."

Click?

"You can save these vaquitas..."

The two click at each other. "Of course we can, dude."

"Will you help me?"

Silence. They're waiting to hear more.

"Each of you will get half of the group, and every day I want you to check in with those members, and tell them if you've seen any nets. Tell them where it's safe to swim. Swim with them for as much time as you can allot each one."

The vaquitas consider it. Anita doesn't know, but one is thinking, "Does that mean I have to share my secret feeding ground?" and the other one is thinking, "But how will I get time to spend with that cute vaqui girl?"

El Jefe gives a deep, growling buzz.

The vaquitas look at him for a moment, then back to Anita. And then they click: "Ok, we'll do it."

* * * * * * * *

Over the next week, Anita settles into a comfortable pattern: after leaving the house, she swims to the Garden and briefly shepherds her quartet. Convinced they're safe, she heads south, where El Jefe and his new deputy El Sud bring her up to speed on the patrols by Vente and Spots.

She can tell that El Jefe is proud of the youngsters. They're reliably making their rounds. So far, only one gillnet was found. The porpoises steered clear of it.

Anita would almost be enjoying herself if it weren't for two nagging feelings: first, she still hasn't encountered enough vaquitas. Her numbers only add up to twenty-five. Is that it?

The second thing gnawing at her: how can she keep this up? School starts in less than two months. Can she rely on the porpoises to patrol themselves?

* * * * * * * *

At the restaurant early the next day, Anita is mulling it over: twenty-five. Is that all?

She doesn't notice that Pedro has crept up to the counter and is staring at her. "Boo!" he shouts, startling her so badly she drops a plate. It crashes onto the floor.

"What do you want?" she asks, barely polite as she picks up the shards of ceramic.

"Can't you tell?" he asks, just on the verge of creepy, and then when he sees she doesn't take it well, he changes his tone. Matter-of-factly, he says, "Coffee and huevos rancheros. Tita, you don't like me much, do you?"

Anita doesn't answer. She concentrates on clearing up the broken plate. "What's keeping Mamá?" she wonders.

"I'm sorry I wasn't nice to you when we were kids." Anita looks at him. "I've turned over a new leaf, Tita." He smiles and she has to admit, the smile seems sincere. "Won't you go out with me?"

"I don't think so, Pedro. But here's your coffee."

* * * * * * * *

EL JEFE

My human daughter is out on patrol. Selfishly, I wish she were here with me.

She is making progress with our language. It is much slower progress than my children made, but that is understandable. It is not her language.

And yet I understand her. The Lord Creator speaks through her, I know.

Lord Creator, please help. I know I ask you for many things. But if she could understand me, she could learn our stories. Surely this is something you want.

There is much to tell her. The legends of the Orca Times. The resulting diaspora and the Lost Ones. And selfishly, of my own family. So they might live again.

* * * * * * * *

Anita remains bothered by the numbers. A new refrain has started in her head, "Where are they? Where are they?" Are there really only twenty-five?

Her mother is running late visiting a supplier; Anita is alone again. Dicing peppers and thinking about the vaquita numbers, she hears someone approach. Looking up, she sees it's Pedro. He gives such a nice smile that she returns it.

"Good morning, Tita. I've decided to come here every day for breakfast, to charm you into seeing a movie with me."

"It won't work, Pedro. I'm busy at the restaurant all summer."

"This place is closed for dinner! What do you do at night? Or Sundays?"

"I'm busy... anyway, what do you want today?"

"The same thing I want every day..."

"I MEAN: what food? What drink?"

"Just coffee today, Tita."

She's just about to ask what's keeping him in town when she hears a voice crying, "Tita!"

Juan Carlos, the older boy who helped keep watch over Lola, comes running up to the counter, his eyes red. It's obvious he's been crying but is trying to hide it.

"What is it, Juan Carlos?"

"They found another one," he says, choking up.

No, no. NO! Anita feels her legs become lead. Sinking, she sits down, and prays it's not one she knows.

* * * * * * * *

The boy's distress shakes her out of her own. Anita rises, walks to the front of the counter, and embraces Juan Carlos. Then she says, "Tell me what you know."

"Some men were talking on the malecón just now. They said a dead vaquita was found, way down on the eastern coast. With ten totoaba… the fish were gutted."

Anita wants to swim to her vaquitas right now. Again she prays, "Please don't let it be one of my friends!"

She gives Juan Carlos another hug, and he hangs on to her. But what can she really do to console him, when she can't console herself?

Finally they part, and the boy turns to go. Touching the shell necklace at her throat, Anita watches him leave. When he's out of sight, her strength breaks, and she begins to sob.

She doesn't even remember Pedro is there. He's been silent the whole time, standing off to one side. Now he goes to Anita and embraces her. A truly sweet comforting hug. "It's ok, Tita, it's ok."

"No. No, it's not," she protests.

After a few moments, she calms down and Pedro asks what it's all about.

"The vaquita. They found another dead vaquita."

Pedro's sweet side is overpowered by his I-know-best side.

"Listen, Tita, you need to forget those porpoises. They don't have a chance. And I'm surprised they're still finding any – my dad thought they were gone twenty years ago. And you know what a smart fisherman he is."

Anita is too numb to even hear him.

He drones on, "Besides, it's not our fault they're dying off. The Americans dammed the river and it's been a death sentence for them. There's not enough fresh water coming in. So don't blame the fishermen. Blame the people who want to live in a desert."

Anita doesn't want to blame anyone. She just wants the vaquitas to survive.

She looks at Pedro blankly. Then she gets up from her chair and says, "I never got you your coffee."

* * * * * * * *

MARÍA

I am frightened. When I came to my restaurant today, Tita was silent. Her eyes were swollen from crying and I asked her about it. In a dull voice she told me another vaquita is gone. It didn't even sound like her. She sounded lifeless. For a moment I felt a panic: Tita will die when these creatures are gone! But that's ridiculous, I know.

I begin to feel I must tell her father.

Tita, Tita. What should I do?

I must speak with her again about calling The Sisterhood.

Tonight I know she will swim all night, counting up her friends to see if any is missing... What a sad and lonely mission.

* * * * * * * *

The kid is having doubts. I heard it in his voice when we talked today.

He thinks he can get out, maybe even thinks that if the totoaba are drying up, his time with us is over. Doesn't he know? It's never over with Shar. He owns us.

I mean, is the boss really gonna let the kid just yammer to anyone about what we've been doing?

When and if we don't need him anymore, we'll let him go. But even then we'll always be watching over him. You know, to make sure he keeps quiet. To make him do the right thing.

We're his family now, aren't we? And what are families for?

* * * * * * * *

Anita swims to her quartet. They don't seem to know. Their mood and energy are good. Should she tell them? She decides against it and tries to keep it from her thoughts.

After a brief visit, she says goodbye. With dread, she heads south.

She is just past the boat landmark when she feels something touching her leg. She looks back, and there is El Sud.

Click, click! The animal smiles at her.

"Hi, Sudi... listen, do you know where El Jefe is?"

Before Sud can answer, El Jefe appears. He also seems lighthearted.

"It must not be one of his herd," she thinks. "Still, I'd better make sure." Trying desperately to keep her mind blank and away from the latest death, she says, "Please take me on full rounds tonight."

El Jefe and Sud nod, and they guide her to join Vente's

patrol. First with Vente, then with Spots, they visit the others. All alive and well.

El Jefe is looking at her, waiting. Finally, she decides she needs to be honest with him, and says, "Jefe, I need to talk to you alone."

El Jefe nods and they swim away, apart from the others.

Anita faces him. Feeling a sob welling up inside her, she cries, "I let you down! I said there'd be no more deaths! But they found another one killed on the beach."

El Jefe stares at her, remaining motionless and silent.

Anita continues, "It's no one I know! Do you know where there are other vaquitas?"

El Jefe stays still. For a long time he just stays in one place, staring at her.

Under his gaze, Anita breaks down. Distraught, feeling she's disappointed him, she turns and bolts away, racing off towards home.

* * * * * * * *

EL JEFE

It is bad news, of course. Very bad.

But I tried to tell my human daughter it is not her fault. I focused all my thoughts into that. But I don't think she understood. She became very upset and left. Poor thing, it is not what I wished.

The dead one must be from the Area. One of the Lost Ones. It is several days since I got report of the nine brethren living there.

No longer nine. Now eight.

It is bad news, and yet: that is not a place we have patrolled. So we are having some success.

But only thirty-three of us are left.

* * * * * * * *

Anita sleeps poorly. Usually she's so spent physically that her sleep is heavy. But that night she's in anguish. Another one gone, and where did it come from?

And was El Jefe upset with her?

Unsettled though she is, she reaches a decision: in the morning, she'll contact the marine mammal sanctuary and get the survey details. Maybe it will reveal something useful for the patrols.

In a corner of her mind, she knows the whole strategy can't last. School is coming. What will happen? If only more of the vaquitas could see well. If only more of the vaquitas were leaders like El Jefe or Sud. If only more of the vaquitas had sense, like Espy and Virgil. If only, if only...

The alarm finally rings. She gets up and finds her mother in the kitchen. Anita whispers, "I'll be a little late for work. I have to call the sanctuary – and we know they don't open until 9:00."

"That's ok, Tita. But I want you to consider what I said. I want you to call for help."

"Help with what?" says Miguel, smiling at them as he comes in for breakfast.

"Oh, I was just telling Tita she should let me know if she needs my help with the tables. Yesterday was so busy she was running off her feet."

"My Tita can handle it," he says, kissing the top of her head.

"Miguel, will you come with me to the restaurant? The ice machine is acting up and I want you to look at it." She winks at Anita: privacy to make the phone call.

* * * * * * *

9:00 comes. Trying not to besiege them – she knows it's a small office – she waits. But impatience gets the best of her, and at 9:04, she calls. Anita's not good at being deceptive, but she tries her best at fibbing. She says, "I'm writing a paper for school. Can you please tell me about the vaquita survey?" She knows this is lame. School's out for the summer.

The man on the phone – is he the one who carried the tarp? – puts her on hold, and a woman answers.

As Anita talks with her, she's sure it's the one who came and collected Lola's body from the beach. Anita has an irrational anxiety that the woman not recognize her voice.

The woman must not have had her coffee yet, because she doesn't even balk at the school paper line. She states, "The researchers wrote the report last month, and they said thirty. It's their best estimate, of course, and it could be plus or minus a few on either side. With the recent deaths, the estimate would be twenty-seven."

The woman continues, "They're almost all in the Refuge... but there are a few to the east, outside the Refuge."

Anita is stunned. How could she forget the eastern area? She heard about it when the report came out.

"Gracias," she says, hurrying off the phone. Then she sighs and asks herself, "How am I going to cover that area, too?"

* * * * * * * *

Entering the restaurant, Anita runs into her father as he's leaving. "Is everything all right, Papá?" she asks, all innocence.

"Fine. I don't know what your mother was worrying about. The ice machine works as good as new. But you're a little late today, eh Tita?" he smiles mischievously at her. He's happy when she can take a break. She seems to do so few fun things anymore.

"Yes, Papá, I was sleepy this morning. Slow to get going."

They say their goodbyes and she dives into work. She's driven in a way she's never been, almost with super-human energy. She has to keep it together: the restaurant, her home life, the patrols. All day, a new refrain persists in her head: "I have to figure out what to do about that new area."

* * * * * * * *

Anita is distracted when she reaches the Coral Garden. Joining Espy and Abuelita, she barely greets them, asking in a panic, "Are the boys ok?!" Espy reassures her they're just off feeding together.

"Thank goodness," says Anita, then gives a hasty goodbye and rockets to the south.

Swimming so fast and with the new area on her mind, she doesn't even notice that Mateo has come alongside her. All of a sudden, she feels herself being lifted. "That way, Mateo," she says pointing, "And thanks!"

Mateo lets her off just before the sunken boat, and swims away. Anita locates El Jefe and is pleased to find him feeding. In their first nights together, El Jefe never ate at all. He must be feeling better. Maybe even hopeful.

"El Jefe, I must talk with you," she says, somewhat nervously. She's worried he's mad at her for the latest death.

El Jefe lifts his head slowly from the sea floor, as if caught in a dream. Recognizing Anita, he swims to her, nuzzling her arm. "I am at your disposal, my child."

Over the next hour, Anita gets a clearer view of the situation. Using yes/ no questions, and snout nods from El Jefe, she learns he knows how many vaquitas there are. Counting with handclap gestures, she learns there are thirty-three vaquitas. She repeats this several times, and it's always thirty-three.

This is where the conversation starts to get hard.

"I know of (four handclaps) close to me, in the Garden... Abuelita is one of them. She's your sister, correct?"

El Jefe nods his snout.

"I know of (twenty-one handclaps) here in the south. That includes you and El Sud and all the vaquitas that Vente and

Spots patrol."

He again nods.

"El Jefe, that means we are up to (twenty-five handclaps)."
He nods.

"Today I learned of an area very far to the east, where the
sun rises..." She almost says, "Outside the Refuge." But how
could he know about such a thing, a human judicial concept?
The sea is the sea.

She repeats herself, "Today I learned of an area very far to
the east... is that where the eight are?"

El Jefe nods.

"Do you hear about them? Do you keep track of them?"

El Jefe says, "As best we can." Anita thinks she
understands: it's far for them to go.

They sit in silence for a little while. Anita tries to cover her
thoughts, because she doesn't want to worry El Jefe. What
she's thinking is: there's no way I can continue my efforts as it
is, let alone add a whole new region.

And she doubts the vaquitas can manage on their own.

* * * * * * * *

EL JEFE

My human daughter just left. She seemed pensive. It makes me
sad. I don't understand it. I think we are making great progress,
and now that she understands about the Area, I know we can
keep all of us safe.

We, of course, cannot go to the Area. That would not be safe.
Our history will not allow it. But she can go, and come up with
a plan to patrol it.

I have great faith in her.

* * * * * * * *

By the next night, she's decided what to do. "I'll ask El Sud. He's loyal and will go with me. The first few nights, we'll go together, and we can establish patrols there."

She heads south, prepared for a very long night of swimming. Luckily, Mateo shows up, giving her a ride and saving her valuable time. As before, he drops her off just before they reach the boat landmark.

She runs into El Jefe first. "Do you know where Sud is?"

El Jefe is disappointed – he had hoped to talk history with her tonight. Her language has improved so much! But he tells her that El Sud is making rounds in Vente's area.

Anita swims off and finds him. "Sud, will you come with me? There's a region we're not patrolling."

Is she imagining it, or does he seem nervous? There's a sense of anxiety, a quivering in the water.

But El Sud loves her and says, "Yes, I'll go."

The two swim off, heading east. Initially they go at a fast pace, but soon Anita notices Sud falling behind. She waits for him to catch up; then they take off again, more slowly. But again, Sud lags.

"What is it, Sudi?" she asks, getting worried. The animal just looks at her with his beautiful eyes, unable to tell her.

They try again. Anita notices there's a huge rock formation below them. She moves to swim across the rocky prominence and head farther east. But El Sud doesn't follow.

Anita swims back to him, and encourages him to join her. He makes a few attempts, goes a few feet, and then he erupts into a piercing cry. The only other time Anita's heard such a noise is when El Jefe gathered the herd together.

Anita rushes to Sud, examining him from snout to tail, looking at his dorsal fin. Is he hurt?

At the surface, Sud lets out a huge gush of air. She's surfaced with many vaquitas, but none can blow their blowhole like Sud.

Anita's wondering what to do next when she sees El Jefe rushing in towards them. Anita is shocked. In their time together, El Jefe has never moved that fast.

"NO!" she feels him crying. He's using his snout to direct El Sud back home.

Once he's sure Sud isn't hurt and is heading the right direction, El Jefe turns to Anita and says, "There is no way you could know, my child. But we cannot go into the Area."

* * * * * * * *

Anita learns there was a time long ago that vaquitas swam like most dolphins and porpoises: together in large groups. Socializing and being together. But then the orcas settled in the Sea and they massacred the vaquitas. "It was the time of our first near-extinction," El Jefe tells her.

To avoid the orcas, they split up, all going their own ways, feeling safe only in small groups. "Even my family – whom I dearly loved – we rarely stayed together. I was with my wife. When our first child came, she went with him. Then she went with the second, then the third. That is how we are."

The Sea Mountains were a dividing line; the eight vaquitas to the east had been cut off for many generations. "We call them our "Lost Ones." We communicate through turtle allies, and occasionally a trustworthy octopus."

And so Anita realizes: she'll have to patrol the Area."But school's coming! And the Area is twice as far from home!"

Could Mateo help? He could only take her so far, otherwise the vaquitas would be scared off.

How is she going to do this?

She spends the rest of the night with Jefe and Sud, but really, she's lost in her own thoughts. She barely remembers swimming in and going home.

* * * * * * * *

Anita wakes up, decided. Her mind figured out what to do while she slept.

She gets dressed for work in her usual: jeans and a plain red T-shirt. Then she opens the top drawer of her bureau.

Digging underneath some socks, she finds the watchcase.

Anita opens the case and lifts a corner of its satin lining. Hidden there is a scrap of paper. She pulls it out and confirms it has a number on it. She slips the paper into her pocket.

She'll call at the end of the work day.

* * * * * * * *

TONY BAI

So my L.A. connection – the one who puts the goods on the planes to China – told me Customs is sniffing him out and we have to lay low.

I asked him why he doesn't just pay them off but he says there's an idealist working there now. God, I hate idealists. Do-gooder types make me want to puke.

So the agent can't be bought off. Bad enough. Worse, he's convinced his team to be more thorough inspecting the cars from Baja. So I can't even drive the stuff up. It'll have to stay in Mexico for a while... Great. Dozens of bladders stored in that god-forsaken town.

The kid is helping me find safe places for them. He doesn't sound too happy about it, but he's doing it.

* * * * * * * *

The work day is over. Anita can't put it off any longer. She studies the paper: there are a lot of digits. "This can't be a Mexican number," she muses, realizing it's got to be the most exotic phone call ever made from her mother's restaurant. Nervously, she dials the number.

The phone rings twice. A woman answers, and Anita explains the situation, that she can't handle it alone anymore.

"We'll send word when to expect help. Thanks for the

73

good work."

The line goes dead.

* * * * * * * *

Anita continues her patrols, not venturing into the Area. She feels too overwhelmed to tackle it.

Two weeks go by. The first week, Pedro visited the restaurant every day. The last time she saw him, he looked really nervous. But Anita was too preoccupied with her own thoughts to pay much attention. And now he's been gone a week and she's barely noticed.

Sweeping the restaurant patio, she thinks ahead to her patrol. She wonders if Mateo will give her a ride. El Jefe caught a glimpse of him the other night. He wasn't happy about it, but calmed down when Anita insisted Mateo was friendly and would not come closer.

Anita locks up and starts to head home. As she walks, she feels an air current close above her hair. Then a gull flies down, landing before her on the street. In an absent-minded way, Anita notices the bird's bright yellow feet.

She moves to pass the bird, but it squawks up at her. Peering down, she sees it has a paper twisted around its yellow leg. The bird lifts the foot, offering it as if he were a customer in a shoe store. Anita laughs, bending closer to remove the paper band.

"Is that hurting you, little one?" she murmurs. Her fingers gently remove the paper but the gull isn't satisfied. It just stares up at her. Only then does Anita glance at it... and then she realizes it's for her.

Nervously, her eyes scan it. The note says, "Be sure to be at the restaurant August 1."

The gull squawks again, searching Anita's face.

"I read it, gracias," Anita states, and gives the bird a tiny salute.

It lifts one wing in reply. Then, its duty fulfilled, the gull takes off, flying high above the sea.

PART II: THE TEAM, THE PLAN

Anita is at the restaurant early. Today's the day. Help is coming. Goodness knows she needs it – with school starting in a month, how will she study and keep her patrols going? And what about patrolling the Area?

Anita isn't sure exactly what she expects... maybe if someone asked her, she would say Dr. Rios would come, or bring a colleague. But breakfast comes and goes and the marine biologist does not arrive.

María knows it's the big day. She wants to be supportive but doesn't want to interfere. "Tita, I'm running to the market. I didn't plan well for lunch."

Anita nods absent-mindedly. It's a weekday, so it should be fairly quiet. She can handle the restaurant alone.

She's idly wiping menus, when she feels her wrist start to ache. She looks up. Approaching the stand is a tall girl about her age, thin, with curly auburn hair, glasses, and very pale skin. She looks American.

"Buenos días," Anita says, her heart starting to beat faster.

"Buenos días," the girls replies. "Are you Anita?"

"Yes."

"The Agency sent me."

"Agency?" Anita wonders. She doesn't say anything but her face shows her confusion.

The girl explains, "The Sisterhood's Intelligence Agency. …Hi, I'm Emily."

She extends her hand; Anita is taken aback at the adult manner of this girl, who can't be any older than fifteen or sixteen. She's wearing a cotton blouse and hiking pants, but it might as well be a business suit.

"Hello," Anita replies, shaking her hand.

"Listen, is it safe to talk here?"

"Yes, while it's empty. My mother will return soon, but she's..."

"Oh, and we shouldn't talk around her?"

"No, no, it's ok. She knows."

"I get it. Sometimes the parents know, sometimes they don't. My mom doesn't know, for instance. I think about telling her – it would make things easier – but she'd worry too much. Plus, I don't want to get her in trouble. She's a veterinarian, and if I have to use some of her animal tranquilizers, it's better if she's kept in the dark."

Anita struggles to keep up. Her English is pretty good, but she's a bit overwhelmed by this newcomer, who not only talks fast, she talks a lot. And what are tranquilizers? She decides the smart thing to do is ask. "What are tranquilizers?"

"Oh, sorry. I have a bad habit of just talking and assuming people always know what I'm talking about. Like last year in physics, I spoke about the CERN experiments to observe the Higgs boson and everyone just had a blank look on their face." Emily realizes this look is starting to take over Anita's face, too. "Right. Tranquilizers are sedatives..."

"Sedatives?"

"...medicines to put people to sleep."

Anita asks why she needs those.

"In our line of work, you have to be prepared for any eventuality. I was working on something at the lab in Costa Rica that might work just as well, but that will have to wait. Anyway, listen, would it be ok if I have some juice or something? It's already been a long day! I logged my 136th and 137th flights this morning and I have to say the 136th – the

Pittsburgh flight to Phoenix – was pretty awful. Really long wait on the runway. It made me wish I could fly... but we can't all have those talents."

Anita is barely keeping up. She points to a pitcher of orange juice and gestures, "Is this ok?"

Emily nods. "Great," she says. "And how about a snack? Anything really. Vegetarian, please."

Anita makes her some bean and cheese tacos, trying to suppress a worry that it's all doomed.

* * * * * * *

Emily and Anita are chatting – or, rather, Emily is chatting at Anita – when her mother arrives, laden with bags of groceries.

"Mamá, let me help you," Anita jumps up from her chair, nearly tackling her mother in an effort to get her alone in back.

In the kitchen, María asks, "Is that who they sent?" María's a kind person but she's finding it hard to believe a girl even skinnier than her daughter – and apparently even younger – is going to help.

Anita says, "Shhh!" and nods. In a quiet voice she says, "She seems nice enough. And smart."

María can hear the doubt. "Be careful, Tita," she says. Anita nods.

They exit the kitchen together, smiling at their guest.

"You must be Anita's mother. I'd say I heard all about you, but the truth is, we didn't talk about you at all. Is this your place? The salsa's delicious. I absolutely love Mexican taquerias. My father studies Mayan culture, so I've been to the Yucatan quite a bit. Have you ever been?"

The two Pérez women shake their heads.

"Oh, it's amazing. Ruins everywhere. Every day it seems they're finding another ruin. If you see a hill, it's a ruin with jungle on top – the natural topography is very flat. Absolutely love that part of Mexico. Though this looks very nice, too. The Gulf of California, huh? Quite different from the Gulf of

Mexico. And yet, many similar species of birds. Maia will tell us more about that, I'm sure."

Emily's off and running. María steals a glance at Anita. She shrugs her shoulders in return.

They let Emily continue talking. She finally remembers she has food on her plate and takes a few bites. "I'm the slowest eater in the world. And I have two older brothers, so you can imagine that I don't get much at meals. Maybe that's why I'm so skinny."

Anita and María are both thinking, "Or making you work it all off with your jaw muscles." But Anita is warming to her. María remains suspicious.

Emily reaches into the satchel at her feet. Out of it she pulls a watch exactly like Anita's. Seeing it, both Pérez women think, "That's reassuring."

Emily sees them looking and says, absent-mindedly into her bag, "Yes, never wear jewelry when traveling. For one thing, it slows you down at the security checkpoint. For another, it makes you a target... Anyway, it's 11:35 a.m., right?" Saying this, she clasps the watch on her wrist. María checks her cheap watch and agrees it is. "Just wanted to make sure. You know how travel can get you all turned around time zone-wise."

Actually, they don't. Neither has ever left their time zone before. But they keep silent and wait for what she has to say next.

"We're meeting the others at La Roca at 2:00."

Anita feels relief wash over her. "The others." Her mother looks noticeably more comfortable. Not that Emily isn't perfectly nice, but...

"How long does it take to get there?"

Anita stumbles over this. It's a basic question but she doesn't know: can Emily swim like her?

Emily, for once, says nothing. She's waiting for a response. She looks at Anita then at María. "Well?" she asks, almost curt.

Flustered, Anita says, "Well, that depends. If we swim..."

"Oh. No. Nope. Can't do that. Yours truly can't swim.

Well... maybe I can swim thirty feet... but then I get panicky. I assumed we'd take a boat – a panga, right? That's what you call them?"

Anita and her mother don't know how to react. She gets panicky swimming? And she's here to help the vaquitas?

María snaps out of it first and chimes in, "Yes, 'panga' – exactly right. Anita, sweetheart, you know your father can't lend you the boat today..." She's looking intently at Anita, really saying, "There's no way you can take his boat, how would I explain that?!"

"Well, I saw a rental place as I was walking in. Can you drive one? I've never done it. I mean, I just got my learner's permit, but that was for a car, not a boat."

Finally on solid ground, Anita says, "Yes, I can drive it."

* * * * * * * *

Thank heavens María accompanies them. Sr. Ramírez will not rent to an underage American ("too many chances for a lawsuit, Sra. Pérez!"), so she signs the papers. She has full faith in Anita captaining the boat. Even if they crashed, Anita could certainly rescue the other girl. Ruining a motor boat is the least of María's concerns. Maybe she was wrong urging Tita to call The Sisterhood and getting her hopes up. Is this Emily really going to help?

"Anita, should I go with you?" María asks.

"No, Mamá. It's ok. Go back to the restaurant – the customers are probably wondering where we are."

María nods and hugs Anita. She turns to Emily and says, "It was very nice to meet you, Emily. Have fun." Walking off, she realizes it was an absurd thing to say. But everything is absurd these days, isn't it?

Emily doesn't even notice. She's eager to get on with the mission. So much to learn, so many problems to solve. She can't wait.

* * * * * * * *

Anita expertly guides the small boat to a crevice in the face of La Roca. It was only a forty-five minute journey but Anita couldn't help noticing Emily got paler and paler. And now her face looks green. She hasn't even been talking.

"Th- that wasn't so bad, was it?" stammers Emily. Scrambling for solid ground, she pitches herself out of the boat. She almost hugs the rock she's so happy to be out of the boat. Only after landing does she realize the surface is coated in bird droppings. "Glad I brought a change of clothes!" Emily says, trying to put a brave face on things.

Again, Anita wonders: "She's here to help me?"

It's very loud. The seals and sea lions are shouting at each other, and seabirds are shrieking. The girls crawl up the rock face to get a seat and a bit of quiet. At the top, they sit on some papers Emily pulls from her bag.

They rest in silence for about five minutes, Emily taking deep breaths and allowing her natural color to return. Much improved, Emily checks her watch. "Not long now," she says.

* * * * * * * *

SHAR PING

My lieutenant just called me. He's a greedy young man, but I understand him.

He reports the Customs situation remains challenging. The new supervisor is an "ethical" man… one apparently satisfied with a meager salary. We'll have to find a way of convincing him otherwise.

Tony also says the totoaba is disappearing. He sounds worried. "What will become of me?" I can hear the whine in his voice.

I don't like whining.

Still, he's been loyal to me.

I told him to sit tight and enjoy the ride. The extinction of the totoaba will drive the prices up. I have bladders stored all over China. I'll release the bladders in dribbles over decades and the price will go higher and higher. It's quite a lovely little racket.

I reassured him there's plenty of work: logistics to oversee, getting the bladders to market, covering the trail.

But I hear the unhappiness in his voice. He's young and wants to be – how do the Americans say it? – "where the action is."

Maybe I'll move him to Tanzania. My team there needs a reliable head since Zhang was arrested... Yes, Tony, maybe I will send you to Africa.

As for the underling – Pedro? – the one trying to leave me... we'll handle him when the times comes.

* * * * * * * *

Anita sits quietly as Emily lectures her on the historical significance of guano.

"Yes, most people don't know how important it was for fertilizer... I mean, wars were fought over bird poop," she says, looking into her lap. Anita is getting used to Emily, and realizes she almost never looks at her when she speaks.

But now Emily glances up, and something catches her eye. She jumps to her feet, calling out with excitement, "I think that's her!"

Anita stands, and follows her companion's gaze. Emily's looking far off, high into the sky to the northeast. All Anita can see are birds. No planes, no helicopters. What's Emily talking about?

With great speed, several of the sea birds approach their rocky home. One of them is particularly enormous – a red and black blur streaking right toward them...

"What...?" Anita doesn't even have time to form the

question. Fast as an arrow, the large figure dive-bombs the island, pulling up at the last moment and landing with a gentle step. The red "feathers" turn out to be sleeves.

"You've really got the landings down now, Maia!" Emily exclaims, rushing to meet her friend.

"Emmy G!" the "bird" calls out with delight.

Anita thought she was weird enough, being a fish-woman. But now she's seen a bird-woman and realizes anything is possible.

* * * * * * * *

"Where have you been, Emmy G?! I thought we were gonna hang out in Pittsburgh!"

Anita just watches the two. It seems like they've known each other for a long time. The birdwoman might be older – or is she just more womanly? She's pulled off her cap, revealing a short afro haircut outlining her beautiful dark face. Her voice is deep and resonant.

"I stayed longer at the lab than I expected... I was working on some things..."

Maia grins and gives Emily another hug, "Can't keep you outta that lab, huh?"

Then she lets go and steps back, to get a look at Anita. With a "what do we have here?" attitude, she eyes Anita from head to toe.

"So, you're the self-made bodhi, huh?" she gives a doubtful look.

Anita recognizes the feeling the look implies. It's the feeling she had about Emily: "Really? Her?" All she can do is give a weak smile.

Breaking into a grin, Maia comes forward and embraces her. "Thanks for the good work, sister," she says. "We heard all about you."

* * * * * * * *

Anita's completely flustered. How do they know each other? How do they know about her? How long has Maia been able to fly?

Her questions will have to wait. Emily and Maia are deep in conversation, and – shockingly – Maia gets in her fair share of words. Which is nice, because Anita could listen to her all day. Such a lovely, comforting sound.

"She'll be late, you know she will," Maia laughs.

Anita keeps watching them, realizing: I feel lighter! It's been ages since I laughed. There's something about Maia... or maybe it's the two of them together... that makes her feel... hopeful? Joyful?

Emily's saying, "Yes, of course, Jess will be late. But we can start planning while we wait for her."

"Naw, let's hear from Anita. Anita, tell us about the vaquitas."

* * * * * * * *

Anita describes the porpoises and her interactions with them. She's pleasantly surprised to find she not only holds Emily's attention, but Emily takes notes.

Maia seems particularly interested in the vaquita language. At one point she says, "I don't think that's one I'll ever get," and Emily gives her a consoling look.

Then Maia checks her watch. It's the same as Anita's and Emily's. "2:30. Not 2:late, as far as Miss Jess is concerned... Emmy G, while we wait for Jess, let's check out the birds!"

"That's a great idea. I already read the Audubon guide for Baja," Emily says, reaching into her bag and pulling out binoculars.

"Me, too," Maia says, then calls out, "Hey, Anita, maybe you can tell us the Spanish names..."

The three girls spend the next half-hour counting and naming dozens of birds. "Some of the same ones as in Costa Rica..." Maia says.

Costa Rica again. Anita realizes they were at the camp

together, and the girl they're waiting for probably was, too. "Chess," she says in her head. "Yess..." The English 'J' sound is very hard for her. She absentmindedly practices it, looking up for the arrival of the last girl.

All three are looking skyward. Maia and Emily continue with the binoculars and their birding, and Anita searches for Jess – as if she's now used to people flying in under their own power.

It's Maia who sees her first. "Emmy, you're not going to believe this..." she says, pushing the binoculars at her friend.

* * * * * * * *

Emily lifts her glasses, and adjusts the binoculars to her eyes. She scans the sky but sees only gulls.

She puts the binoculars down to re-orient herself. Jess will be coming from the north, right? From California. Emily checks the compass on her watch – yes, she has north right. She looks again to the northern sky. Nothing.

She looks to Maia, who's pointing. Not at the sky, but at the horizon. There, out on the sea, is a speck.

Emily lifts the binoculars up again. "Oh, wow..."

"Maybe she swims like me!" Anita thinks. Eagerly, she asks if she can look.

Maia and Emily are just staring at each other. Silently, with an astonished look on her face, Emily hands Anita the binoculars.

Laughing Maia says, "Only Jess."

And through the binoculars Anita sees her: a young woman on a surfboard.

Over her shoulder Maia explains, "Jess surfed here from Southern California."

* * * * * * * *

Anita doesn't think she can hear them right. Her mind cries out, "There's no surfing this far north in the Sea of

84

Cortez!" But there the girl is. Greedily, Anita keeps the binoculars, watching this tiny figure in a royal blue wetsuit gliding towards them, beckoning the waves to form and do her bidding.

She looks through the binoculars until she feels she must let the others have a peek. Then she looks at Maia, and then she looks at Emily.

And now Anita knows. Help truly has arrived.

* * * * * * * *

EL JEFE

Today has been a strange day. Strange but wonderful. The waters shimmer and dance. Elation is everywhere around me.

After the high sun, I was at my private feeding ground – what my sister calls my "study" – thinking if there were any way we could help the totoaba. I rarely see them anymore, but the Elder tells me a small number are hiding in the Area's Kelp Forest. I was considering asking my human daughter to include them in our patrols.

Preoccupied in thought, I surfaced to breathe. And then my eyes beheld a large bird flying to La Roca. A bird I have never seen before.

She landed on the island and the island seemed to pour out strength.

I let this fill me and made rounds to my tribe. All were calm and quiet, letting the strength carry them.

A while later, the sunny sky became brighter than I have ever seen it. As if the Creator itself was taking a sunbath. The waters pulled this way and that, but it was not frightening. Our tribe bobbed back and forth with the sea, in a dance of great healing energy.

Things are still now, but the water remains happy.

I will ask my daughter what she knows of this.

* * * * * * * *

Anita, Emily, and Maia watch as Jess rides her board in; as she gets closer, Emily and Maia call out, "There's a sight for sore eyes!" "Jess! Good to see you!"

The surfer rides her board right to the base of the island, coming in among dozens of sea lions.

She clambers up the rock, takes off her small backpack, and gives her two friends big hugs. The three of them laugh and chat for a minute or two. Anita feels out of place. She tries not to stare, taking in Jess with her small slim figure and light brown shoulder-length hair.

But then Jess swings her body to face her and exclaims, "Anita, great to meet you!" and gives Anita a tight embrace.

"You, too," Anita replies. She feels shy, and yet comfortable, too.

The four girls settle on the ground, Jess asking if anyone has any water. "I'm all out – it was a long ride!" she laughs. Her green eyes sparkle in the sun.

Emily grabs an aluminum water bottle from her bag and offers it.

Between gulps, Jess asks, "So, G, have you figured out desalination yet?"

Emily shakes her head no and Jess explains to Anita, "One of the many problems Emily is working on... water is getting more and more precious."

Anita, quiet as always, just tries to keep up with the conversation. She nods, pleased she understood.

Putting the bottle down, Jess says, "Alright, so here's how I see it: we have just one month to get this situation in hand. Then we have to go back to school. So... Anita, can you tell us what's going on? How many vaquitas are there? And *where* are they?"

Emily starts in, "Anita was just telling us..." when Maia looks at her kindly but firmly.

"Sorry... go ahead, Anita."

"There are thirty-three. There are twenty-five in the Refuge..."

Jess asks, "That's where nets are illegal, right?"

"Yes. Then there is another place... the Area. It is... more far... farther from my home, and I could not patrol it. So I called for help. Eight vaquitas live there." She adds, "In the Area, it is legal to use nets."

"Tell us more. Do the vaquitas interact with you?"

"Yes. They think of me as a friend... as a sister." At this, Tita looks down at her hands, slightly embarrassed.

But Jess beams, and is just about to say, "That's awesome!" when Emily demands, "What about the nets... have you seen any up close?"

"Yes. There are different kinds... but they are all hard to see, especially at night. That is when I swim, because I help my mother during the day."

"Well, you've done a great job... there haven't been any deaths since you started, right?" asks Jess.

Feeling slightly ashamed, Anita says, "Three have died. Two were in the Refuge and one was in the Area. It was the... the last one dying that made me know I must call for help."

Jess looks at her kindly, then says, "Anita, one other question..."

"Please... call me 'Tita.'"

Jess smiles. "'Tita'... I like that... Tita, the Vaquita..."
They all laugh.

"Tita, you said you've seen the nets up close. Have you ever swum into one? I mean... could you get caught in one?"

"No, I haven't. But I could. They are very hard to see."

* * * * * * *

87

Jess, Emily, and Maia sit quietly, chewing over what Tita has told them.

Finally Jess stands up and says, "Before we get into strategizing, I want to take a few moments of silence. I want to pray that the Earth approves of what we do. I want to pray that the Creator approves of it, and gives us guidance. And I want to pray for our so-called enemies... people who are behaving badly... out of fear and delusion."

She reaches for Tita's and Maia's hands, and Emily completes the circle. With their faces to the sun, the girls let the light shine onto them. Tita isn't sure what to make of it all, and yet she's not embarrassed.

After several minutes, the barking of the sea lions becomes especially loud, and Jess breaks the silence with a joyful laugh. The circle disbands and the girls take their seats again.

Jess begins, "Emily, tell us what you've been up to since we got the word to come."

"Well, I've identified several knowledge gaps. Let me start with the facts we know: totoaba are caught here in the Sea of Cortez (aka the Gulf of California), and their bladders are sold in China, primarily in Hong Kong and Guangzhou markets. The bladders' alleged benefit – and it pains me to say, it's all so ridiculous – is improved skin texture. That's because bladders are essentially bundles of collagen. Collagen is the elastic protein that's the foundation of skin.

"Collagen breaks down with aging. Some uninformed people think eating collagen will replace their own stores and keep their skin young. But that's idiotic, because the proteins get digested – first by stomach acid, and then farther along the gastrointestinal tract."

Here Emily takes a breath.

"Everyone with her so far?" Jess asks, especially looking at Tita.

"I'm ok," Tita laughs. "I understood most of it!"

Emily resumes, "So... the knowledge gaps are: where precisely are bladders being sold? How do they get from the Chinese airports – and sea ports – to the markets? We understand from arrests here in Mexico and in the U.S. that runners smuggle it from fishermen here, cross the border, and deliver it to contacts in Southern California." Tita nods hearing this. It fits her town's experiences.

Emily says, "We have much less information on the Asian side. To address that, I've established contact with two bodhi sisters, in Hong Kong and Guangzhou. They're investigating who sells it, and who the regular customers are."

Tita interrupts, "Excuse me, what does 'boaty' mean? Something to do with the sea?"

Jess and Maia laugh, creating a chord of gentle music. Then Jess explains: "Bodhi: b- o- d- h- i... comes from 'bodhisattva'..."

Maia interjects, "It means a being who's here to relieve suffering."

* * * * * * * *

Tita barely has time to process the weight of all this before Emily continues, "So that's some of the intel I'm trying to gather. But the big question is: how are we going to stop the totoaba bladder trade?"

They hope it's a rhetorical question. She has the answer, right?

But Emily just looks at the circle of faces, hoping for suggestions. So Jess starts, "Well, I know you have some ideas about the nets, but I was also thinking Tita and I... with our patrols..."

Tita's ears prick up: "our" patrols?

Jess continues, "...we could find the poachers and track them... and get the authorities involved."

Emily simply says, "It's not going to work."

Tita agrees. First of all, she doesn't think she's brave enough to risk confronting poachers. Secondly, she doesn't trust the authorities. Their corruption has been undermining conservation efforts for years.

Emily adds, "The authorities don't go after the real villains.

89

The people who've been arrested have been low-level: the runners, a few poor fishermen. They're making peanuts compared to the businessmen. And even when anyone gets caught – which is rare! – they only get a slap on the wrist."

"People don't care enough," Tita suggests, wrestling with a thought she often has.

Jess shakes her head, disagreeing, "People care, they just don't know. It's just a few delusional people doing this. Most in this town want the vaquitas... the vaquitas could be a great boost to this town's economy... let alone its culture."

Emily nods, "Yes. That's right. But I'm afraid the delusional people have the upper hand right now, and the vaquitas and the totoaba don't have time for them to become enlightened."

* * * * * * * *

The sea lions are loud but silence still manages to fill the group. Silence and worry.

Finally Emily offers, "Ok, I have two ideas. First, as Jess knows, I've been working on some net coatings – non-toxic, of course – that will make the nets much easier to see. Easier for fish and vaquitas to see. Not easier for humans! We can't have the fishermen noticing something weird about their nets!"

Tita's curiosity is piqued and she listens intently as Jess asks, "I know you thought about trying to sabotage the nets when they're manufactured... are you still thinking that?"

"No, I looked into it: new nets are made in dozens of Chinese factories. There's no way our Chinese sisters could sabotage on that scale. Besides, lots of nets are already here. I read a 2011 article about a vaquita death. Using the photo, I traced the net design, and it was manufactured in the 1990s... No, if the coating works – and it's a big if – we'll have to go around and hand-paint the nets here."

Jess looks concerned. "That's an awful lot of girl-power..."

"I know."

Maia asks, "What else, G? You said you had two ideas."

Tita doesn't hear the next part, because she's contemplating what Emily just said. She's proposing causing nets not to work. Even legal fishermen would have a hard time earning money to feed their families. But... if the idea buys time for the vaquitas... it would be worth it, wouldn't it?

* * * * * * * *

Emily has been speaking for about two minutes when Tita comes out of her own thoughts. She holds up her hand and says, "I'm sorry. I am lost a moment ago... sometimes the English is hard for me."

Jess intercedes, "It *is* a little hard to follow. You lost me with the "anti-collagen antibody" stuff. Can you say the second strategy again?"

Maia groans, "The condensed version, G. Please."

Emily gives a mock-hurt look, then says, "Ok, the short story is this: women buy these bladders to reverse aging. So I thought we should do something to the bladders to induce aging. Hit them where their vanity is, and they'll stop buying.

"For both the net coating and the aging idea, I asked the Agency to send me supplies – a full lab, really. When I arrived today, I went to check into my apartment, and everything is already there. I just have to set it up. Anyway, we'll see. They're tough problems."

Maia just stares at her. Then she says, "Induce aging? For real?"

"Yes. I think there's a good chance I should be able to induce wrinkles. And gray hair."

Maia gives a whistle of admiration, then shakes her head in disbelief.

Tita thinks, "I should pinch myself." Girls that fly? That surf from America? That cause gray hair?

Unfazed by the girls' astonishment, Emily says, "It won't be easy. But it's a fantastic puzzle."

* * * * * * * *

After they joke about causing a new fashion trend of looking old, Jess says, "Ok, so Emily's going to work on the nets and on the pro-aging substance..."

Maia laughs, still shaking her head, "'Emmy G's Pro-Aging Cream'!... it won't exactly fly off the drugstore shelves! But here's hoping it can save the vaquitas!"

"You got that right!" exclaims Jess. Then she gets back to business: "Tita, you'll continue your nighttime patrols. I'll do daytime patrols..."

"On your surfboard?" Tita asks.

"No, I think one grand entrance is enough... I don't think we need all of Baja talking about the sudden unexplained appearance of swell, and a cute Little Surfer Girl... No, I'll swim... like you."

Tita lets it sink in: Jess is like her.

Jess continues, "I can swim like you...but my fish vision isn't great... so I'll stick to daylight hours. Which leaves..." she turns her body slightly, "you, my dear Maia."

"I already have a plan," Maia says.

"I do, too. Let's see if our minds are Of One," Jess jokes.

"Get to know these local birds and use them as spies?"

"You got it, sister."

* * * * * * * *

Jess explains, "We'll need as many allies as possible, looking for nets. It may be a while before Emily's concoctions are ready... The birds here should be on our side, but we can't assume anything."

Maia says, "Let me start with the brown pelicans. I had some success with them at Camp. Even Mrs. Bixby said I did a good job."

Tita's face shows her confusion, and Jess laughs, "Mrs. Bixby is Maia's language teacher. She's really tough, so if she complimented Maia, that's high praise!"

Emily just nods in agreement, a slightly cowed look on her face. Tita thinks: they all seem a little afraid of this Mrs. Bixby.

Emily stands up and surveys the surrounding water with binoculars. "There's a small flock of pelicans about five hundred feet away."

Maia stands up, takes the binoculars from Emily, and looks. Then she transforms her melodious voice into a series of deep squawks and hoarse grunts. Tita just stares at her. Jess watches Tita, laughs and then smiles at Maia. "Yep, Mrs. Bixby would be proud."

Slowly, three of the pelicans turn their trajectory from the open sea to come in to The Rock.

* * * * * * * *

As Maia talks with the pelicans, Jess turns to Emily and says, "G, how far along is the coating?"

"I have a prototype in my bag," she says. "I thought we could test it today on the fish around here."

As Maia squawks back and forth with pelicans, Emily opens her satchel and pulls out a small segment of net. She holds it up in the sunlight; it looks like a clear hairnet.

"Here it is," she says, and passes it to Jess. Jess takes the piece and rolls it between her hands and holds it up to the light. Then she hands it off to Tita, who also examines it.

"Nothing special, right?" Emily asks. "That's good – 1 like I said, we don't want the fishermen to notice anything." Then she asks, "Your vision hasn't transformed much, Jess?"

"No. I can only see biofluorescence once in a while. Like I said, I'll need the sunlight for my patrols."

"Tita, what about you?"

"Yes. I could do the testing."

Emily looks excited, "I was going to ask if you swam using a flashlight... No, huh? Your eyes have a filter effect? Reliably?"

Tita feels like Emily would like to get her in an ophthalmologist's exam chair right now, and put her through a battery of tests. Embarrassed, she says, "Yes... it started three years ago... and it's stronger now. I see better than the vaquitas do. I don't use my flashlight very much."

Emily smiles with excitement, "So we'll test it on you first, but then we'll need to test it on them..."

Tita agrees, silently worried the plan won't work. Sure, Spots and Vente would see a coating... maybe Sud... but the others? The coating had better be really bright.

* * * * * * *

Maia finishes talking with the pelicans, bowing to them as they fly off the island.

Jess asks, "Well? What did you find out?!"

"Those are some cool birds." Maia shakes her head, delighted. Then she gets serious, "They said they're really happy we're here, that some of their relatives have been killed"

Emily cuts in, "They dive into the nets to catch the fish, then get stuck, too."

"Yeah, so they're eager to help. We talked about the range and they said their flock could cover the Refuge. But they don't know of any brown pelicans in the Area. They said there were some gulls over that way and maybe I should try to recruit them."

As she says this, Jess scans the sky with the binoculars. "Well, there's no shortage of gulls... I see about twenty right over there."

Emily takes the binoculars, "Those are herring gulls – common seagulls. I'd suggest we recruit yellow-footed gulls. Aside from a few that go to the Salton Sea up in California, the Sea of Cortez is their only home. They should be eager to protect it. Herring gulls, on the other hand, probably don't care as much... since they live everywhere..."

Emily continues to scan the skies. After a few minutes she calls out, "There's one! A yellow-footed gull!"

"I don't know Gull, but I bet it's a dialect of Common Seabird. Let me try that." Maia releases a series of bird cries very different from the grunts of Brown Pelican. Her piercing shrieks easily capture the gull's attention; the bird turns, and comes flying down to them.

Jess giggles as its feet hit the ground. "It looks like it's wearing little yellow rubber boots," she says quietly to Tita.

Tita starts to laugh but stops when she sees the bird looking at her. At first she thinks he's mad at them, but then it dawns on her: "You're the one who brought me the message!"

The bird bows his head, "Yes, good to see you." Then he turns to Maia. They talk animatedly.

Finally Maia says to the girls, "This is Cornelius. The Sisterhood told him we'd be coming. He leads a flock and they're happy to patrol the skies above the Refuge – or the Area – whatever we need!"

* * * * * * * *

They continue plotting strategy until the sun starts getting low. Tita realizes she has to get back. "I must go home now."

Emily stands up and says, "I should go, too, and get to it. Lots to do." She brushes off her clothes as best she can. "Including change," she says.

Maia gets up. "I don't care if you are covered in bird poop..." and the two embrace, though Maia does avoid the worst of the mess. They stand arm in arm, rocking happily.

Jess says, "I'll go with you guys... If it's ok with you, Tita, I'll join you on patrol tonight."

Tita nods, yes, of course. Inside, she feels mixed emotions. Does she really have to share her flock? To hide her confusion, she asks Maia, "Are you ok? Staying here alone?"

Maia smiles, "Are you kidding? This is luxury camping. Best views in town. And my Emmy G gave me some sandwiches and some water. I'm all set. I got all these birds to talk to and get to know."

Jess, Tita, and Emily head down to the panga. "Enjoy the island, lovely," calls Jess over her shoulder.

"Say hello to the vaquitas for me!" Maia calls back.

As they're climbing into the boat, Tita notices a sea lion lounging on Jess's blue surfboard, at home as it could be. "Look," she says pointing it out to Jess and Emily.

"Awesome!" Jess cries, giving a thumb's up to the sea lion. "Take care of it for me!"

The sea lion barks back in return.

* * * * * * *

Tita drives the boat back towards town, but, at Emily's urging, stops the motor mid-way through the journey.

"Let's test the net!" says Emily. "Jump in, Tita. There are no other boats around!"

Tita looks uncomfortable.

Jess asks, "What is it, Tita?"

"I don't have a swimsuit." She came from the restaurant and, for once, is in regular clothes.

Emily is about to chime in, "Go naked. Nobody's here! Aren't you eager to see if it works?!" But before she has a chance, Jess says, "I have one, here in my backpack. We'll turn around while you change."

Tita gets into the suit, then flips over the side of the boat. She briefly notes that it's been ages since she felt the water on her skin – no wetsuit today. Then she puts her hand out.

Emily gives her the netting, and Tita heads deep underwater with it. Though the day is fading, she wants there to be as little light as possible.

She's gone for about ten minutes. Jess waits calmly, but Emily starts to get worried. Is she ok? Can she really swim without breathing? But then Tita's face emerges, glowing in the red sky, a big smile on her face.

"I took it into a cave… It's bright green! I can see it very well!"

Jess gives Emily a high five.

* * * * * * *

They return the panga to the boat rental, but it's a bit awkward: Sr. Ramírez is clearly perplexed. Three girls? There were only two before. Where did this girl come from, the one

96

with the smooth hair? Another American? But she does better with boats: she looks fresh and happy, while the curly-haired one is a worrisome shade of green.

He looks at Tita, who gives a nervous chuckle in response. "We have to go, Sr. Ramírez. You see: the boat is fine."

"Yes, yes... well, good night, Tita."

The three girls walk off, Jess breaking into giggles. "The look on his face!"

Thrilled about the net, Emily recovers quickly as they walk up the beach to the malecón.

"We will part here." Tita says. "Do you have money?" Emily and Jess nod, and Tita tells them where they can get something cheap to eat.

"I guess I'd better not go to the fanciest place in town," Jess laughs. "Unless they have a Wetsuit-Only policy in the dining room..."

"I have some clothes at my place," Emily says.

"Way too long, I'm afraid, Miss Leggy."

"We are the same size. I can lend you some," Tita says.

"Thanks. I think most of my time will be in the water. But I may need to take you up on that... So, should we meet at 10:00 tonight?"

Tita replies, "10:30?" That should give her just enough time to see her parents off to bed.

"10:30 it is. And G, what will you do tonight?"

"I have plenty to keep me busy. I have to set up the lab."

Jess and Emily hug Tita, then they go their own ways.

* * * * * * * *

MARÍA

Tita's eyes are gleaming. I cannot wait to ask what happened at La Roca. But her father wanted to play chess with her. I'm not able to get a minute alone with her.

We're being so unfair to Miguel. When things are more settled,

I'll ask Tita if we can tell him.

But everything is alright. I feel it strongly. Leaving my restaurant, the very air seemed to say, "Everything is well. Go home to your family and be at ease."

I see that peace in Tita. It has been a long time coming.

* * * * * * * *

Tita arrives about fifteen minutes late. And if she hadn't lost the chess match on purpose, she'd be even later. When her father finally went to bed, María whispered, "How was it?" All Tita could do was smile and say she'd explain in the morning.

Jess is staring at the sea when Tita approaches. There's something about Jess that makes Tita nervous, but also makes her happy. She can't explain why, but she wants her to be proud of her. And yet, like Tita, she's just a sixteen year old girl.

Jess breaks into a wide smile when she realizes Tita has arrived. "Sorry, I'm a bit out of it... I was just thinking of my sister Amy. She loved the water even more than I do, I think."

Tita's not the interrogating kind. She doesn't ask anything, but she knows enough English to understand "loved" is the past tense. What happened to her, she wonders?

Jess shakes her head, as if to clear it of the cobwebs of memories. "So, tell me, Tita. When did you learn you had it? The ability?"

Tita sits down next to Jess. The sand is still warm from the hot August day. "Three years ago. And you?"

"A month!" she says, laughing. "I'm still freaking out a bit."

Tita laughs with her, "Yes, it is a lot. It's a wonderful gift... but... sometimes I feel lonely."

Jess nods, "Definitely. That's why it's so good to be with you... and with Maia... she can fly and she just takes to that like it's no big deal... for me, the flying is harder..."

Tita just listens. So Jess can fly, too? Hmmm. Then she asks, "And Emily?"

"G?... You know why we call her 'G'?"

Tita shakes her head.

"There's a book for kids... *Curious George*. Do you know it?"

"The little animal?... un mono..." Tita fishes for the English word.

"Right, the monkey," says Jess. "Emily's family calls her George. Because when she was young she asked a million quesions. But then she learned everything so she hardly asks questions any more... you may notice she talks quite a bit..."

Ever polite, Tita doesn't say anything.

Jess just looks at her face and laughs. "It's ok, we all know it. She knows it, too! Anyway, Maia met her and put it together: Emmy G, or just G for George."

"And does she have any special abilities?"

"You mean super powers?" Jess looks at her like: We're crazy, right? Then shakes her head. "Well, actually, yes. Her brain's like a computer... well, better than a computer... because she's not just brilliant. She's compassionate."

"'Compassionate'? What does that mean?"

"It means she cares."

* * * * * * *

Tita and Jess spend a magical night together, covering all of Tita's favorite haunts. First she takes Jess to the Coral Garden, and introduces her to Espy and the boys.

"I am so pleased to meet Tita's best friend," Jess says to Espy. Abuelita swims in, delighted that Jess said the exact right thing, and clicks a warm welcome to her.

Then, the girls head south. Above the landmark of the capsized fishing boat, El Jefe swims up to meet them. Tita isn't sure how he knew about Jess, but he clearly did, and is obviously excited to meet her.

She says, "El Jefe, this is Jess. And, Jess... this is the leader of the vaquitas."

"El Jefe, it's an honor to meet you. Tita thinks of you as a second father."

If vaquitas could blush, Jefe's gray face would be very pink right now. He seems to puff out his chest and bows low. Then he gives a series of clicks. Tita translates: "He thanks you for coming. Now, he says, he'll call his deputy, and they will take us to see the other vaquitas here."

El Jefe makes some loud clicks, and soon El Sud arrives. After more introductions, they all tour the southern Refuge. Vaquitas come out to greet them as if they were a diplomatic delegation. The normally shy creatures click and buzz and kiss the girls with their snouts, eager to make them welcome.

Eventually the girls have to go. With full hearts, they say goodbye to El Jefe and Sud, and head back to Tita's beach. They reach the sand exhausted but ecstatic.

"Tita, meeting those vaquitas was... unbelievable! And that's the most breathless swimming I've ever done!" She gives Tita a hug and says, "My friend, we're going to do this. Those vaquitas are in good hands. Now all we have to do is find out what's going on in the Area!"

Tita nods happily. She was silly to worry – patrolling with a friend was wonderful. But it's time to turn to practical affairs. She asks, "What will you do now? Go to the apartment? You need some rest."

"You're right about that. But I'm so tired I don't even feel up to flying to Emily's. I might just sleep in the sea."

"You will be safe in our sea." Tita wrings out her hair and adds, "Just don't sleep on the beach. That's not allowed. The police patrol the beaches."

Jess giggles, "They patrol the beaches, we patrol the sea..."

Tita laughs. "I will be at our restaurant by 7:30 – it's right over there," she says, pointing down the malecón. "You'll see me at the counter. Come there and get some breakfast!"

"I'll need it!" They give each other another hug and Tita heads home, and Jess heads into the water.

* * * * * * * *

Pedro is back. After a week away, he shows up at the restaurant. Tita is squeezing oranges in the kitchen, wondering when Jess will arrive, when she hears him calling.

She walks to the front counter, stopping along the way to pour him a coffee.

"Tita! I missed you!" he says, smiling warmly at her.

"How have you been, Pedro?"

"Great! I just had a charter... a guy who develops real estate in Arizona. He said he's always going to use me as his captain... and if I ever leave fishing, he might hire me at his company!"

Tita is just about to ask, "Why would you want to leave the sea?" when she sees a petite figure walking down the malecón: Jess in her wetsuit, heading to the restaurant.

"Buenos días," Tita says nonchalantly when Jess enters. "Can I help you?"

"Just... just some orange juice, please." Jess is behind Pedro, so he can't see her make eyes to Tita, eyes that say, "Can you get rid of him so we can talk?"

Pedro doesn't take any notice of Jess. He's too absorbed telling Tita his big plans. Finally he looks at his watch and says, "I have to go! See you tomorrow, Tita!"

Watching him leave, Jess says, "Is he a friend of yours?"

"Pedro? I don't know. When I was young, he teased me. He's nicer now, but... I don't really trust him."

They watch him walk down the malecón. Once he's out of earshot, Jess says, "I'll eat breakfast, and after I digest, I'm going to swim out to the Area today."

"You must be careful. There are many boats in the Area."

"Better they don't see me, huh?"

* * * * * * * *

Jess finishes her meal, and the girls are talking animatedly when María arrives.

"Mamá, this is Jess." Without even thinking about it, Tita says, "She's our leader."

Meeting the girl, María feels an odd sensation. She finds herself starting to bend forward. Then the girl smiles and gives María her hand. Straightening, María snaps out of it. Who bows low to a teenager?

"Welcome to Baja," María says warmly.

"Thank you."

"Mamá, you must be so eager to learn what we are up to..."

"Yes! Am I allowed to know?"

Jess answers, "Of course, Sra. Pérez. And we'd appreciate your input!"

* * * * * * * *

During the morning's slow moments, Tita and Jess bring María up to speed, and discuss the best plan for patrolling the Area.

Jess says, "Maybe I will just set up camp with Maia on The Rock... since the Area is pretty far from town... or maybe your orca friend could take me..."

María turns to Tita and asks, "Orca friend?!"

"It's ok, Mamá. Really. It's ok."

María just shakes her head. Walking back to the kitchen, she says to herself, "When I finally talk to Miguel... I think I'll leave the orca out. He doesn't need to know *everything*."

* * * * * * * *

It's almost the end of the work day. Washing dishes, Tita's thinking of Espy, how graceful she is when she swims. Then she hears her name.

"Tita!" It's Emily.

Tita leaves the sink and goes to greet her friend.

"Tita, I've brought the net with me. Do you think you can test it on the vaquitas tonight?"

"Of course."

"I was thinking first you can test it again here, in the

102

bathroom... with the lights off."

Surprised, Tita says, "But it worked yesterday..."

"I want to make sure the fixative works."

Tita says, "Oh, I see. Of course."

Emily hands her the segment and Tita takes it to the bathroom. When she emerges, Emily can see the bad news on her face.

"Was it still at least a little green?" she asks, hoping.

Tita shakes her head. "I'm sorry. It does not glow at all."

* * * * * * * *

Emily looks crestfallen. Tita wonders how to console her when they hear someone approaching. The girls look up: there's Jess, still in her wetsuit.

"Hey!" Jess says, then sees their faces. "What's up?"

Emily answers, "Well, the net coating that worked yesterday doesn't work today – it faded completely. That's obviously not helpful... nets can be out there for a while."

Jess looks solemn, and says, "Well, I have some news, too. The good news is that I met all eight vaquitas of the Area. The bad news is that I found eleven gillnets."

"And those were just the ones you could see," Emily adds.

"Right... just the ones I could see..."

Emily looks thoughtful for a moment and then says, "It's ok. I've got lots of ideas. There are different fixatives I can add."

Jess asks if it's too late for tacos. Tita says of course not, and encourages Emily to have some, too.

The three sit together, feasting on bean and cheese tacos. Emily is getting more and more excited, talking mostly to herself, naming chemical compounds Jess and Tita have never heard of. At one point, Jess catches Tita's eye and winks.

After they finish eating, they clean up. Emily asks Jess if she wants to stay with her that night, but Jess says, "I'm going to The Rock to hang with Maia. I need to hear what the yellow-footed gulls are seeing... Tita, do you know how long the vaquitas can go without breathing?"

Tita shakes her head, "I'm not sure. They like to come up every few minutes when we swim together."

Emily states, "Sperm whales can manage ninety minutes... but there's no way a vaquita can do that. I'm guessing about five minutes. That's what a harbor porpoise can do."

Jess sighs. "So even if the gulls see something and alert us, we might not get there in time."

There's a heaviness to their leaving the restaurant. Tita feels overwhelmed. The net coating didn't work... There are nets all over the Area... Will their patrols work? And how long can they keep up the patrols anyway?

Noticing her concern, Jess takes Tita's hand and says, "It'll be ok."

Then she steps back, smiles at them both, and says, "Alright, I better get to The Rock."

"Should I get a boat?" Tita asks. "I can take you there. You have... swam...?" She looks to Emily.

"Swum."

"...you have swum so much."

"You forget..." Jess winks at Tita again, skips a few steps down the street, then leaps into the air. "See you soon!" she calls from on high.

Emily and Tita watch her until she's just a dot in the sky, then they look at each other, and laugh. "Just you and me, kid," Emily says. They walk arm in arm until they reach the street for Tita to turn.

"It'll be ok," Emily says, echoing Jess. "I've got lots of ideas."

* * * * * * * *

With wild hair and bloodshot eyes, Emily comes to the restaurant the next morning.

"Did you sleep?" Tita asks.

"No, I was working on the net coating. And then... well, I started thinking about the aging idea. To pursue it, I realized I need some totoaba bladders."

"Shhh!!" Tita says, kindly but firmly. Looking around, making sure no one overheard them, she adds quietly, "We must be careful when we talk about that."

Emily makes a "Whoops! Sorry!" face and whispers, "Do you know where I can get some?"

Tita thinks about it, then says, "Let me call the marine mammal center."

* * * * * * * *

María usually closes at 4:00, but today, after gently rushing the last customer out, she closes at 3:30.

"Ready?" she asks.

"Thank you, Mamá." Tita's especially grateful because she knows that her mother will come back and clean alone. Most of the closing work was left undone. But the center is only open until 5:00.

They walk the short distance to the Pérez home. Coco greets them, very eager to meet Tita's new friend.

Emily strokes his sandy brown fur.

"Well, hello, sir. And what are you? A mutt?... I'm sorry: I should say, a mixed breed? My mother – who's a veterinarian – that's a doctor who takes care of dogs... she says mutts... I mean mixed breeds... are the best dogs of all. Personally, I think any shelter dog is the best..."

Coco isn't really listening. He's enjoying the stroking too much. Besides, she uses too many words!

The three humans get in the car, Coco crying when they don't let him join them.

María drives Tita and Emily to a nondescript cement block building on the edge of town.

"Are you sure you can handle this alone?" she asks her daughter.

Tita nods.

"I will be back here at 5:00."

Tita and Emily watch as María drives away. Without

hesitation, Emily heads into the building. Tita trails behind.

They enter the small lobby and a woman in an inner office calls out in Spanish, "I'll be right there." Tita feels a flush of embarrassment, but nothing like she felt earlier on the phone.

Out comes a short somewhat stocky woman of about fifty. She looks kindly at the girls and extends her hand first to Emily, "I am Sofía Castillo, the manager here." Then to Tita, "And hello again. We seem to keep meeting. I hope that school report of yours turned out well." Her eyes have a mischievous look, much as her voice did on the phone today. She seems nicer than that day on the beach. Maybe Lola's death really had been hard on her, and she didn't want to show it.

"Thank you so much," Tita says apologetically.

Sofía Castillo brushes it aside and gestures for the girls to follow her into her office.

When the girls are settled on the loveseat, she leans back in her chair and says, "So... this is what I know: I have two teenaged girls asking me for bladders... each of which is worth, what, eight thousand dollars? Ten thousand dollars?"

They sit in silence, waiting. Tita sees that her lips are crinkling at the edges, like she's trying to be serious but wants to smile.

"I could very easily tell you we have no bladders here. Why would we have any? Do you think fishermen drop off bladders and totoaba bodies, and ask us to put them back together?"

She continues, "No, no they don't. In fact, if we regularly kept totoaba bladders here, we'd be robbed faster than you can say, 'Easy money.'"

The woman seems to be enjoying having a chance to speak English, which she does fluently. Plus, they get the feeling she likes them. Even though she's protesting, she's on their side.

"But... when I hear the name 'Dr. Rios' I take notice. So after Anita called me, and told me Dr. Rios wants this, I called Dr. Rios. And she said, yes, give these girls whatever they want."

Here she leans across her desk and peers at Tita and Emily. "What I want to know is: why?"

The girls still haven't said a word, and they don't start talking now.

"Not for me to know, hmm?" she laughs.

Silence.

"Well, you're in luck. We have two bladders here. Frankly, we haven't known what to do with them. They were confiscated when that young male vaquita was found."

Here Tita interrupts and asks, "The one on the eastern coast? The most recent one?"

Sofía shakes her head, "No, I don't know much about that case. The authorities in Sonora are dealing with that. I'm talking about the one from the southern Refuge."

"Odi," Tita thinks to herself. "Sina's son."

Sofía continues, "Just between us: there were two young fishermen out that evening who got caught. Apparently they work for a guy named Vicente Méndez. He wasn't with them that night. Anyway, the police didn't arrest the two because they agreed to be informants. From what I hear, the authorities mean it this time when they say they want to end this business."

Tita soaks all this in. It's good to hear that other people are making the vaquitas and totoaba a priority.

"So, we have two bladders... and you're welcome to them. I probably don't have to tell you this, but: keep them safe. That's a lot of money in a small town like this."

She gets up from her desk and asks, "Ready to go get them?"

* * * * * * * *

She leads them through the office complex, to a walk-in freezer located next to a large tiled room. Pointing to the room, she explains, "That's where we treat the animals that come here, mostly seals and sea lions, and turtles. And where our veterinarian performs operations. And, I'm sad to say, autopsies."

The girls look into the room. It has a cold clinical look to it, but they know a lot of love is there, too.

They turn their attention back to Sofía, standing beside the freezer. Gesturing to it, she says, "Usually this is just where we keep the fish we feed our animals. But today I must warn you that we still have the body of the vaquita I mentioned. We perform autopsies but not on the vaquita. Those are sent to the Scripps Institution of Oceanography up in San Diego. They have a vaquita expert there."

Tita dreads asking but feels compelled. "Is that where Lola went?"

Sofía looks at her, "The young female you found? Yes," she breaks her gaze with Tita and says, "Sadly, the day we sent her body out became the day this young boy died." As she says this, Tita realizes the job takes its toll on the woman. That must have been a heart-breaking day of work.

Sofía resumes, in a business-like tone, "It's some consolation that – Lola as you call her – will help science understand vaquitas better. I gather that they might even try to capture some of the eggs from her ovaries... who knows? Maybe someday they'll be able to make vaquitas in a lab..."

"That would be horrible!" Tita cries.

"It may be the only hope," the woman says, resignedly but not very convincingly. She isn't sure how she feels about it, and in any case, doubts it could work.

Even Emily, an advocate of Progress says, "It's almost impossible to bring an extinct animal back in the lab. We have to save them here, in their own home."

Leaving the topic, the woman makes ready to open the heavy door.

"Please, before you do that..." Emily says, taking up Tita's hand. "We'll take a moment of silence for the boy in there, and Lola..."

"...and the totoaba," Tita says.

"And the poor food fish," Emily says.

The three women bow their heads in silence.

After a long minute, they look up, and the woman throws her body into the task and pulls open the heavy door. A blast of cold air greets them and they enter the freezer.

Sofía goes to the back of it and takes out a flat cardboard box.

Tita glances at the middle shelf, seeing the body of the vaquita. It looks so small. Was it really that small? Truly, was it a baby? Or has it shrunk in death?

Emily's eyes take in every inch of it. She's never seen a vaquita.

Sofía asks if they're ready to exit. Emily says, "Tita... I hope you don't mind... but I think I should examine this. If Sra. Castillo allows it. Maybe it will help guide our strategies."

The woman nods, giving her permission. She has no idea what "strategies" these girls could have, but she believes in them.

"Please, just don't take anything from it. We're due to ship it this week to Scripps, and the specimen must be intact."

* * * * * * * *

Emily puts on gloves and Sofía does, too, helping her carry the vaquita to the exam room. There, Emily takes out a tape measure and a notebook from her bag, and records various lengths. She's especially interested in the placement of the eyes and their relation to the snout.

Tita averts her gaze, but eventually decides she must look. If the vaquitas suffer, she must suffer, too.

"His name was Odi," she murmurs. She stares at him, waiting for the pain to come. But it doesn't hurt, because this creature barely seems like the animals she loves so well. His spark is long gone.

Tita prays his soul is somewhere else. She prays that Lola's soul is somewhere else, in some beautiful safe sea where Espy will find her someday.

Emily continues to measure the body, then gets her camera and takes photos from every angle. Finally, she spends a great deal of time looking at the eye sockets and the eyes themselves. Frozen beads at this point, not the soft buttons that melt Tita's heart.

Closing her notebook at last, Emily says, "I think I'm all done."

Tita just wants to get out of there.

* * * * * * *

In the car, Tita is quiet while María chats with Emily about the sights to see outside of town.

"I'd be interested to see the cacti in the Valley of the Giants," Emily says, alluding to the enormous cardón plants in the surrounding desert.

"Yes, they are beautiful, in their strange way."

Emily shifts in her seat, the thawing box cold against her thin pants.

They get to her building and Emily clasps the box to her chest. She gets out, thanking Mrs. Pérez.

"¡Hasta luego!" she calls to them, then heads inside.

María turns to her daughter and says, "Are you ok, Tita?"

"I saw the southern boy's body, Mamá. It was so strange."

María turns off the car and looks at her.

"It wasn't even scary. It just: it wasn't a vaquita. It was gone." Her voice starts to break as she asks, "Will they all end up like that?"

Her mother listens, knowing how hard it's been. She's been crying herself a lot lately.

Tita continues, "I know everything dies. But for a species to come to an end? Completely gone?" she shakes her head. "I don't think I can take another vaquita death, Mamá. We're trying. But I don't know if it will work."

Her mother is silent for several moments, and then says, "I think Life will help you, Tita."

She turns the engine back on and starts to drive, then begins to sing softly.

After a few minutes, Tita joins in, and her mood has lifted by the time they pull up to their house.

Before getting out, she says to her mother, "I know you

worry about keeping things from Papá. But this time it really is a good thing he didn't know. That box Emily had? It's worth more than this car."

María just shakes her head at this latest improbable news. She puts her arm around her daughter and they enter the house, Coco not knowing which to greet first.

* * * * * * * *

That night, Tita asks El Sud to take her to Odi's mother.

Sud is surprised by her request, but readily agrees. He and El Jefe have been worrying about Sina. It was bad enough when she lost her mate, but now she rarely eats at all since the loss of her son. She grows thin before their eyes.

They swim a short distance then Sud clicks, "There she is." Tita is shocked by how frail and listless the vaquita looks.

Tita approaches her, and tries to explain she has seen Odi, out of the water in a building. She tells her that his body remains beautiful. It will be studied and used to protect the vaquitas.

She can tell the vaquita doesn't understand. What is it "to be studied"? And what can it mean that he is out of the water? What is a "building"?

Tita drifts in the water, letting the vaquita's confusion wash over her. Has she made a mistake? Should she have left well enough alone? Tita has little experience with death, but thought it might be important for his mother to know she'd seen his body. Isn't that what people mean by closure?

She doesn't know. But she does know that this mother will never see her little one in this sea again.

So she says the only hopeful thing she can, and hopes it with all her heart: "He is in the Great Ocean. You will see him there again someday. But you must eat and take care of yourself. He is protecting the vaquitas and you must do so, too. He hopes you will have a brother or sister for him someday."

Sina listens intently. For many minutes, she and Tita just sit there, bobbing on the waves. The moonless night is dark company but Tita feels a spark of life re-entering the vaquita. Sud looks on, hoping she will be alright.

* * * * * * * *

Emily comes to the restaurant the next day just as the lunch rush is slowing.

"Give me a few more minutes," Tita tells her. It's been a busy day, but she hasn't felt frazzled. There's a lightness in her mood, a background optimism that she helped Odi's mother last night.

Holding her satchel close, Emily sits at a table. After Tita has settled two checks, she walks over to her. "Can I get you anything?"

"No, thanks. Listen, I brought a new net segment. I worked on it all night and into this morning. Today I'm going to start on the bladders. But I want you to test the net tonight," she says. "Can you check it out in the bathroom? Make sure it's at least working now?"

"Of course." Tita glances around. The few remaining customers are busy eating. She puts her hand out, and Emily places it into her palm.

Tita heads to the bathroom. Inside, she keeps the light off. The net glows a neon green.

She puts it in her apron pocket and walks back to Emily. "It's good."

"That's a relief."

* * * * * * * *

Leaving the restaurant, Emily calls out, "Wish me luck with the aging process!"

Tita smiles at her and waves, thinking that's good advice for life. Then she helps her mother make fish tacos for a party of six that's arrived for a late lunch.

* * * * * * * *

Maia's Gull is coming along. With the patient help of Cornelius, she's learning the nuances of the shrieks that separate it from the screeches of Common Seabird. In between lessons, she gets reports from the pelicans looking after the Refuge.

Jess is happy to get a break from the noise, and spend her day swimming in the sun-dappled sea. She's becoming very friendly with the Area Eight. Their communication is limited – they're not as bright as the Refuge vaquitas – but she tries to tell them all will be well.

Yellow-footed gulls whirl above, occasionally breaking her peace with a call when they see a gillnet.

* * * * * * * *

That night, wearing the net piece around her waist, Tita swims to the Garden.

Espy greets her, nuzzling her cheek, asking, "Where have you been?"

Then she looks down the length of her human friend and makes several agitated clicks.

"You see it, Espy?"

Espy is happy to see Tita but isn't happy to see the net. She doesn't want to get too close. She swims at some distance from Tita the next hour, and backs away when Tita tests Leo and Virgil. They can see it at about five feet.

Tita leaves her friends, and swims southwards, putting the netting back around her waist.

She spends a happy three hours in the south, talking with El Jefe. He tells her about his mother and father. His quiet clicks lap at her ears as the calm waves lap at her body. It's a relaxing night of friendship in the sea.

Eventually she realizes it's time to go home. She says goodbye to Jefe and starts heading north, meeting Vente along the way.

"Vente! I have something to show you! This should be easy for you!"

She looks to her waist to unwind the netting; even as she does, she can tell the color is fading.

"Can you see this, Vente?" she asks, swimming back ten feet from him, her hope dimming with the net.

Only when it's at four feet can he see it.

"He did better than that with the regular net," Tita thinks. "Emily's going to be so disappointed."

* * * * * * * *

Meanwhile, working in her apartment, Emily barely gives the net a thought. She knows Tita is out testing it but her mind has turned to something else. After a day cooped up with the problem, she's come to the conclusion: "It's the bladders, stupid!"

They can only stop the trade if they stop the demand. That's classic economics. The net idea? Emily still has faith she could make an effective dye, but has zero faith they could coat all the nets in Baja.

And even if the net coating works, what would that do? Lower the supply of bladders, which would only drive up the price! Then the poachers would try even harder to catch totoaba.

"No. We have to stop the demand. It's the only way."

Emily tries to throw herself into the mindset of a totoaba bladder customer: "I have to be ignorant, selfish, and shallow," she harrumphs.

But she checks herself: that isn't what the Society is training her for. A real solution can only come from empathy.

"Ok, so *confused* people... they think looking young will make them happy... so they're certainly not going to buy it if it makes them old before their time."

She heads to the kitchen – now her lab – and begins looking through the boxes the Society sent.

She reaches for a tube marked "anti-collagen antibody" and thinks about her idea.

[(The following is for anyone interested in immunology.

114

Everyone else can skip it.) Emily's theory: Adding anti-collagen antibody to the bladders will cause the formation of one big protein complex: anti-collagen antibody attached to bladder collagen. Once this complex reaches the customer's bloodstream, the cells of her immune system will recognize it as foreign. Then the customer's cells will make antibodies to attack the foreign substance. Because there is a collagen end to the foreign complex, the customer's antibodies would attack both the big foreign protein complex, and also her own collagen. This would damage her skin, causing wrinkles.]

"But they prepare the bladders in soup... how am I going to get this antibody to stay stable in hot soup... and stable in stomach acid?"

On her laptop, she searches "protein stability in boiling acid." Up comes "thermophilic bacteria."

"Awesome!"

She puts the kettle on to make a pot of tea. It's going to be a long night.

* * * * * * * *

The next morning, Tita is dreading the arrival of Emily. She knows she'll come, she can sense it.

"She's going to be so disappointed," she says aloud.

"What, Tita?" her mother asks.

"Emily is going to be so disappointed, Mamá. The net didn't work." She's just about to explain when they see Emily approaching. It looks like she had another late night.

Tita decides the best thing is to just say it right away.

"The net faded again." Tita braces for her reaction but there's a pause and she isn't sure Emily heard her. "Maybe it's my English?" She says again, "The net... it didn't work..."

"Oh, that's ok. I've given up on that idea. It's got to be the bladders, Tita. Could I have some eggs and toast? I need fuel. It's going to be a big day."

* * * * * * * *

Emily says goodbye to Tita and her mother, who barely have a chance to answer, they're so busy with breakfast. It's Friday and many tourists are in town for a long weekend of fishing.

Once things finally slow down, María asks what that was all about.

Tita explains, and María looks conflicted.

"I don't like that net idea. I understand it, of course. But it isn't right to do that to the fishermen."

"Yes, Mamá. It's for the best it did not work."

* * * * * * * *

It's not going well.

After a full day of research and theorizing, Emily's come to the conclusion it can't be done. Well, theoretically it's still possible, but practically and morally, it's not.

"So much for rapid aging," she sighs unhappily.

"What else?" she asks the walls of her apartment. "Nausea? Projectile vomiting? Explosive diarrhea?"

She's mulling these over but dissatisfaction gnaws at her.

In frustration, she turns on the TV.

Her spirits perk up slightly when she finds a childhood favorite, *The Wizard of Oz*. Even better, it's dubbed. "Well, at least I can see how my Spanish is," she says, throwing herself on the couch. Across from her, on the kitchen counter and table, the mess of her experiments mocks her. Syringes, flasks, tubes, and pipettes are strewn everywhere.

Behind her glasses, Emily's eyes have a glazed look as she barely follows the antics on the screen. "If I could just find a way to put the antibodies in nanotubules..." she thinks, going back to a concept from earlier in the day. It's an idea she's already rejected, but her mind is stuck on it, not having a better one.

"...y tu perrito también!" ("and your little dog, too!") screeches a dubbed-over Margaret Hamilton.

Something about the scene grabs her. Emily bends closer

and peers into the pixels.

The she starts to laugh and exclaims, "That's it!" She grabs her laptop and starts searching. Excitement drives her fingers, one search leads productively to another, and the idea takes shape. The pieces in place, she just needs to decide on re-stocking her lab.

Several hours and many cups of tea later, she has her list together. She places a call to the Agency.

"Hi, this is Emily, in Baja. I need some supplies."

As she's finishing, she says, "That last item? I'll call my mom. She'll send it to the U.S. office and you can forward it to me. She thinks I'm in Costa Rica... besides, I don't think she can get plant material through to Mexico."

* * * * * * * *

TONY BAI

The Idealist is still screwing everything up. Even though we have plenty of bladders here, my L.A. contact refuses a hand-off. Which means I don't get paid. He says LAX is inspecting everything right now, and Long Beach is even worse. Yi has always been a coward, but I gotta admit, I don't want to take chances at the border myself. Apparently the Idealist oversees that staff, too.

So... looks like I have to start finding out more about this guy. See what his life's like. Any kids? One needing expensive medical care? Or one who's a future Einstein looking at a pricey college?

Look for pressure points... negotiating points.

Or maybe just do it the old-fashioned way: arrange a small accident on his way to work.

* * * * * * * *

It's 2:30 the next day and Tita and her mother are putting dishes away when Emily comes to the stand. She seems very pleased about something.

"Sra. Pérez, would it be ok if I stole Tita away? I want us to meet the others at La Roca."

María smiles and says, "I wish I could go, too!" When the girls start to invite her, she shakes her head. "No, I will have an afternoon date with Tita's father."

"And Coco?" Emily laughs.

"And Coco."

* * * * * * *

"My mother signs for it – see here, her note? Have a good day, Sr. Ramírez!" Tita smiles her most dazzling smile and pulls the boat down the sand.

Sr. Ramírez has a good sense of humor and is just going to let this play out: surely it will all become clear? Why Tita needs to rent a panga when her father has a perfectly good one? And where the not-seaworthy American friend came from?

Emily actually does better this time. She can even hold a conversation. "How was your patrol last night? No problems, I hope." Her voice seems to ring confidence. Tita can tell she has big news.

She answers, "It was good. The vaquitas seem to know some people are trying to help. They're not quite as shy as they were."

"I hope they stay shy from nets!" says Emily. Then she asks, "Can you show me how to pilot the boat?"

* * * * * * *

Emily's in a triumphant mood when she steers the boat in near The Rock. But not so triumphant she wants to risk harming the creatures gathered there, so she gives control back to Tita.

Tita gently brings the panga to the base, and anchors it.

"Here we go," Emily announces, jumping onto the rock face.

"Hey, Sammy," she calls out. The sea lion barks back in return. As ever, lounging on the surfboard.

"He's going to miss that when we go," Emily laughs.

"Yes," Tita says, sad to be reminded of their leaving.

"Maia! Jess!" Emily calls up. "It's me and Tita!"

All they hear is a loud bird call, then Maia sings down, "Just practicing some Gull. Come on up! I'll send Cornelius out to get Jess."

* * * * * * * *

"How's it going?" Tita asks Jess when she finally arrives.

She smiles at Tita knowingly. They recognize they're rare company: the only two humans who have ever swum with vaquitas.

"Oh, just another day at the office," she says, winking, and Tita knows she means: "All is well, and, by the way, it was amazing."

Then Jess turns and says, "Ok, Emily, what's the news? How's the net coating coming along?"

Emily answers, "Tita already knows: it's not going to work."

Maia and Jess look at each other with concern. Jess thinks, "Are we going to stay doing these patrols forever?" Maia wonders, "How on earth am I going to explain staying here to my mom? School starts in less than a month!"

Emily then rushes in, a torrent of words. She's going so fast that even Jess and Maia can't keep up, let alone Tita.

"Back up, G!" Maia orders.

"Sorry... let me start at the beginning... it'll help me make sure I'm not missing anything obvious..."

* * * * * * * *

"As you know, it was my plan to sabotage the nets. But we tested them, and the best one I made was a coating that lasted eighteen hours. Which is no small feat, and I might use it for some other purpose. But even before that, I had doubts about the idea."

Maia chimes in, "Yeah, I wasn't sure it was ok to do that to the fishermen."

Jess: "Yes, and I wasn't sure we could ever do it at all. There are so many nets here..."

"Right. Those are major flaws. But the biggest flaw is that it would've done nothing about demand. Idiots – excuse me, Jess – *ignorant* people would still want the bladders... So that brought me back to the aging idea, which seemed like a slam dunk."

Here Tita looks confused, and Jess says, "A slam dunk means a sure winner... it's a sports term..."

"Oh, yes, basketball," Tita smiles. "Go on, Emily."

"Induced-aging seems perfect. People buy the bladders for their appearance, so if we hit their appearance, and they learn it's the bladders' fault... no one would want them. And I could work with the Asian bodhis to push the Internet P.R. campaign... to spread the idea that bladders cause aging."

"P.R?" Tita asks.

"Public relations," Maia explains. "Getting the word out... going viral."

"Going viral... that's funny," Emily chuckles to herself. The other girls are left out of the joke.

Emily resumes, "So, it was my hope that I could inject the bladders with antibodies to human collagen and human melanocytes – they're the cells that make pigments in the hair... well, it was my hope that I could cause wrinkles and gray hair."

The others are thinking, 'It *was* my hope'? Is Emily saying it's not going to work?

Emily stops her monologue. She pauses, then asks them, "Do you know anyone with diabetes?"

They all nod. Maia says, "My grandmother has it."

"And does she take insulin?"

Maia nods.

"Do you know why she has to inject insulin? Instead of just taking it as a pill?"

Maia pauses for a moment and says, "I never thought about it. But since you're asking me... maybe... like our first day here, you said collagen would get digested in the stomach... same thing for insulin?"

"Right. It's hard to administer complex proteins in oral form. And insulin is a protein. So are antibodies. I was trying to solve how they could stay stable... first they'd have to survive the soup..."

"The soup?" Tita asks.

"Yes, the customers prepare fish bladder in soup."

Tita realizes she never thought about what they actually did with the bladders.

"So first my antibodies would have to survive heat... and then they'd have to survive stomach acid... But then I looked into it and I was reminded of some of the coolest creatures on the planet! Have you guys heard of thermophilic bacteria?"

Jess: "Yeah, those are the ones that live in hot springs."

"Not only do they live in hot springs, they live in sulphuric acid! And researchers are finding ways to mimic their proteins, the proteins that can survive that. So I got really excited about using those to protect my proteins..."

The other three wait. Obviously a "but" is coming.

"But then I hit a brick wall."

The girls lean forward to hear it.

Emily looks at their eager faces. Inspired by Socrates, she asks, "Anyone know what the brick wall was?"

Silence.

"Diabetes is your clue."

The three look at each other and lamely try to discuss it for a minute or two, but finally Jess says, "Just tell us. What was the brick wall?"

Emily loves them too much to be disappointed in their mental laziness. Besides, she's delighted with her own success. She spells it out for them: "The brick wall was — even though

I'm mad at these people, and even though they probably deserve it – I can't do them permanent harm."

The girls all react at once: "Permanent harm?!" "Wrinkles and gray hair – seriously?" "The vaquitas are dying!"

Emily smiles shyly. "It's not that. You're right: the sooner they stop caring about their looks, the better. No, I'm not worried about making their outsides look old. I'm worried about triggering an autoimmune disease, like diabetes or rheumatoid arthritis. I'm afraid my antibodies could do that. I don't know for sure, but it concerns me."

Jess and Maia and Tita understand. If they trigger the body with these external antibodies, maybe the immune system will get all out of whack. And so they realize: the aging idea is out. They feel like the air is getting heavier. Is there any hope?

Emily takes a breath and continues, "So then I thought, ok, I can't do that. What about having the bladders cause some unpleasant things, like gas, or vomiting, or explosive diarrhea?"

Jess giggles and Maia says, "Sounds like it's what they deserve."

Emily replies, "Right. And even though it's possible it could make someone sick, it's unlikely it would endanger them..."

The three are getting excited about this idea, and about to descend into some major potty humor when Emily holds up her hand, "But I didn't think it would send a real message."

Maia forgoes the joke she was about to make about bladders usually being for #1 and not for #2, and instead listens as Emily says, "I mean, maybe the buyers would think they just got a bad preparation, or that one of the other soup ingredients was spoiled."

The girls aren't disappointed. They can tell Emily has some other solution. They're leaning in to hear.

Emily looks around the circle and says, "And so... to quote Maia... I've decided... after a little help from the Wicked Witch of the West... that we are going viral."

* * * * * * * *

There's a bit of discussion as Emily prepares to make her final revelation. Jess and Maia first have to explain to Tita who the Witch is. ("Ah, from *El mago de Oz.*") Emily takes some sips of water, relishing the moment, giving off a strong "Darn, I'm good" vibe.

The others quiet down and Emily gives a look that says, "Ok for the maestro to continue?"

They nod.

"So... the human papilloma virus... anyone know about it?"

Jess and Maia both nod. After all, didn't they get a vaccine against it?

"That's the one that causes cervical cancer," Jess answers.

"HPV#16 and HPV#18 cause cervical cancer. Do you know what HPV#2 and a bunch of other types cause?"

Maia laughs, thinking about the witch, "Warts!"

Emily nods her head in delight. "We're going to make those totoaba customers the wartiest people in China!"

* * * * * * * *

Elation suffuses the group. They're laughing and hugging, convinced that Emily's plan will work.

After a few minutes of dancing on The Rock, to the music of seagull shrieks, Jess laughs out, "Tell us more, G."

"Well, the beauty of it is that there's no permanent harm. Warts are easily treated... but it's not like it's pleasant to get a bunch of them. And I've chosen two strains: #2, which causes common warts – these are usually located on the hand, but the inoculation I'm making up will overwhelm and hopefully affect the face, too. And I'm choosing strain #29, which causes filiform warts, which are specific to the face."

The she says, "For an added touch, I'm going to add a little bit of Pennsylvania Pride... I'll tell you more about that, later."

"How long do you think it'll take, G?" asks Jess.

"Well, I've ordered supplies from the Agency. Once they come, I can get started making the solution."

"Then what? How are we going to get it into the bladders

on sale in China?"

"I've already thought about it."

Maia gives a look that says, "Of course she has."

"There's one other beautiful thing about human papilloma virus... and that is it only infects humans. Normally, in fact, it can only persist in humans. But I'm pretty sure I have a technique to stabilize it..."

They can tell another long explanation is coming...

"...it would be hard enough to ship infectious material to China – but it can be done, obviously. Labs throughout the world share viruses with one another. And The Sisterhood is sending me the virus as we speak."

Jess asks, "Can't The Sisterhood also ship your solution?"

"No, we don't have long-distance jets. Even if we did, a big jet couldn't take off from the short runway here. So say we used commercial airlines… that would involve lots of innocent people in the delivery chain, and then somehow we'd have to get the solution from airports into the bladders at markets..."

Tita is trying to keep up. There's a lot of English flying by. Jess, meanwhile, gets an inkling. She turns to Maia and says, "I think I know where this is heading..."

Maia nods at Jess. Then she says to Emily, "You're gonna need some birds, aren't you?"

* * * * * * * *

Tita looks at Emily, as if to say, "Can you please tell me what these two are talking about?"

Emily explains, "Birds would be the perfect couriers. We'll put small vials of solutions on their backs to carry... and even if the vials break, the virus won't hurt them. Then, they can use their beaks to puncture the bladders and insert solution."

Jess asks her, "What do you think, G? About thirty birds?"

"Thirty sounds about right."

Jess asks, "Maia, can you pick thirty of your strongest and most trustworthy birds for this?"

Maia stares straight ahead, pondering the request. She

turns back and says, "I don't know about trustworthy. Trustworthy would be nice. But what we really need are pirates. Vain pirates."

* * * * * * * *

Maia strides over to her small pile of belongings and finds her phone. The others sit, wondering what she's doing.

Maia starts a Skype call, at the same time explaining to the girls, "As you've seen, I've been relying on brown pelicans and yellow-footed gulls for our recon missions. I can't praise them enough. They've been selfless... but I'm afraid they won't do... hold on..."

They hear faint scratchy noises coming through the phone.

"Hold on, Mrs. B, let me put you on speaker... ok, you're on Skype... say hello to Jess and Emily..."

The girls give a shy wave to the screen as a feisty "Hello!" emerges. Why does it always sound like she's rebuking them?

"...and meet Anita."

Tita looks into the phone as it's put under her face. She's about to say hello when she's taken aback... there's a green parrot staring at her.

She looks up, and Maia laughs. "Yes, that's Mrs. Bixby... she's a parrot. A green macaw, to be exact."

Maia takes the phone, sparing Tita the long tirade that constitutes Mrs. Bixby's greeting to her.

Maia then turns from the others, squawking back into the phone, talking with Mrs. Bixby. After a few moments, sensing the girls are eager for an update, she says, "Hang on," and puts the phone down.

"Let me explain: the birds I've worked with can't do the migration we need. It's way too far. But there's another bird that I think will work. And I gotta get Mrs. Bixby to help me trap them into helping us. I speak Seabird but not fluently enough. Plus, I just found out she knows these guys I'm talking about..."

Maia and Mrs. Bixby squawk back and forth for about

125

another five minutes. A very large smile is coming to Maia's face.

She puts the phone down and says, "I think this is gonna work... Hold the line, Mrs. B (squawk, squawk.)"

She turns up the volume on the Skype call, and says, "Go ahead, Mrs. B." A screeching cacophony pours out of the phone. And then Mrs. B stops, and Maia impersonates (im-bird-onates) her, repeating her note for note.

Slowly, the sky begins to fill with large black birds. Emily recognizes them – she has seen a few over their stay here. But never so many together.

Pointing to the unique red pouch at their throats and their split tail feathers, she calls out, "Magnificent Frigatebird," identifying them for the other two girls.

"Shhhh! Don't say that! They might hear you!" says Maia.

Emily looks to Jess and Tita and mouths, "What did I say?" Jess shrugs her shoulders.

Mrs. Bixby screeches out from the phone again, and Maia repeats it. Unmistakably, the birds are being lured in. They're all having the same thought: "What's this? A female calling to us? That never happens! We usually have to do all the work!"

One by one, they fly down onto the island, standing very close together, and close to the girls. All told, there are forty-five of them. They're turning their heads this way and that, looking for the females who have been calling to them.

With occasional help from Mrs. B, Maia says the following to them, in Common Seabird:

"Greetings, frigatebirds."

Frigatebird is a dialect of Common Seabird, so they understand her. A few clack their beaks back at her.

"Some call you Magnificent Frigatebirds."

A few self-satisfied squawks of agreement.

"But are you really?"

Obnoxious screeches start up, the birds scratching at the ground, plumes rising. Itching for a fight.

"What I know... is that you steal food... you never find your own..."

Low murmurs and squawks.

"...you steal it from other birds... chasing them down so they'll give it up... even making them regurgitate so you can have it... from what I hear, we should call you Pirate Birds..."

Agitated clicks and squawks, feathers ruffling.

"...or Thief Birds..."

Real irritation now, as the flock gathers unto itself, getting louder in its complaints. The very largest bird steps forward and screeches at Maia.

"What did he say?!" Jess asks.

Maia says under her breath, "He says we didn't come here to be insulted."

Then she immediately squawks to them in a softer tone, "I've heard all that... and yet, you're such beautiful birds..."

Happy squawks in reply.

"... such strong birds... you fly over the open sea... and no one has solved the mystery of your migration..."

Here the birds are bobbing their heads at each other, and some are blowing up their red throat sacs. Very proud of themselves.

"...I've heard it said that you're champion fliers..."

The head bobbing grows in earnest...

"...though, of course, not nearly as impressive as the legendary bar-tailed godwit."

A full-on symphony of screeches. An outcry of protest. Not the bar-tailed godwit! No, not that!

"Yes, the bar-tailed godwit... so small... so unimpressive looking... that little bird holds the record for the longest nonstop flight EVER..."

It's like she's scratching her nails across a blackboard. The frigatebirds are incensed. How dare she compare them, such handsome black birds – has she seen their tail feathers? – to the drab godwit. That frumpy little shorebird. It's lucky it never comes down to these parts. They'd show it a thing or two.

Maia holds her hands up and makes a "calm down" gesture, then continues her spiel:

"Seven thousand one hundred miles – SEVEN

THOUSAND ONE HUNDRED MILES – in nine days. NINE days. Without stopping to eat, without stopping to drink, without stopping to rest. Who among you could do the same?"

The frigatebirds have worked themselves into a frenzy. The leader seems to be negotiating with them.

Emily thrusts a piece of paper at Maia, whose eyes get bigger as she reads the calculation there. Emily nods encouragement at her.

The leader shrieks back at Maia.

"Yes? You think you could do it?" Maia asks, hoping her voice has the right taunting sound. The number Emily's asking for is pretty astonishing.

Screeches of agreement.

"Well, how about going even a little farther, and a little faster?" Maia glances at the paper, then asks, "Hmmm? How about seven thousand five hundred twenty miles... in seven days?"

The birds are agreeing, not even thinking about it. Nothing matters except their reputation; they haven't even stopped to think why they would want to do this.

"If you could do it... you would truly and forever be Magnificent Frigatebirds."

* * * * * * * *

The birds are excitedly talking among themselves, each trying to puff its neck more than its neighbor.

Maia takes a minute away to confer with the other girls. She explains everything she said to the birds. Jess and Tita just look amazed, but Emily's face has a worried expression.

Noticing it, Jess asks, "What is it, G?"

"Well... I hadn't even thought of it, what with all the excitement of my idea... but... these birds are going to need a lot of calories for this trip... they should have at least a few days of gorging to fatten up... the godwits usually prepare over several weeks..."

Jess announces, "Looks like we'll be throwing a feast for the frigatebirds."

* * * * * * *

It's a lively conversation among the four girls as Tita pilots them all in the panga, heading back to shore. They're excited by the plan, but there's a lot to arrange.

Sr. Ramírez is just staring at them as Tita brings him the key. Surely there were only two girls. Now there are four? Where did these other two come from?

"Good night, Sr. Ramírez," Tita smiles, as the other girls hurry away from his rental stand.

She runs to catch up with them, and a chorus of laughter reaches Sr. Ramírez.

* * * * * * *

They split up on the malecón, Emily heading off to her apartment to continue working on the plan. The other three plot how they can get the provisions for the frigatebirds.

"My parents should still be out," Tita says. "We have a small cart at my house... and I will get the key to my father's boat..."

The three walk to within one block of Tita's.

"I will go first," she says. "If it's ok, I will come back for you."

After a few minutes, she returns, signaling the other two to come. They walk in silence to Tita's house.

Coco is in the yard when they approach. He stays calm and watches the two new girls. Tita bends to pet his head and says in a low voice, "So Mamá decided not to take you with them? She wanted a real date with Papá, hmm? Well, Coco, these are my friends. This is Jess..."

Jess steps up and Coco gives her his paw.

"...and this is Maia..."

Then he gives his paw to Maia.

129

"They are here helping me, Coco. If you ever see them, do not bark. That's a good boy."

The three girls and Coco enter the house, keen to stay out of the earshot of nosy neighbors.

Tita, who rarely jokes, says to them, "I love my town, but here we have a saying: 'Un pueblo pequeño, un infierno grande.'"

Jess, who speaks some Spanish, laughs, but Maia doesn't get it. "Just because I can speak Bird doesn't mean I can speak Spanish!"

Tita explains, "It means: 'A small town is a big hell'!"

Maia laughs heartily, asking, "Everyone's in everyone else's business, right?"

"Sí. Right."

* * * * * * *

In the kitchen, over a snack, Tita tells them where they can go for supplies: "There is a grocery store five blocks from here, it is open for a little longer... the restaurants on the malecón will have fish, too."

She gives them a key, explaining where the Pérez boat is kept at the beach. "You can keep the key until Monday. And then you can make a copy at the hardware store. It is close to the grocery. Tomorrow, I will be with my father, and I can keep him away from the boat."

Then she walks them out, stopping at a shed outside the house. She unlocks it and removes a hand cart.

"Only my mother uses it. Keep it all week. I will tell her."

Maia and Jess thank her, then hug her goodbye. They're just about to go when they hear the tiniest whimper. Jess turns around. "How could we forget?" She bends down and gives Coco a kiss, and says, "Good night, señor."

* * * * * * *

After they leave, Tita gets out of her work clothes and into her wetsuit. Coco just stares at her. He stares at her for so long she finally stops, one Neoprene sleeve still to get on, and asks, "What is it, my love?"

He's silent, but she hears the answer in his body language.

"No, Coco. I'm sorry but you can't go with me. What would Papá think if you were gone when he gets home? Mamá already has to make up an explanation for where I've gone! No, Papá needs you here."

The dog leaves the room, as if to say, "This is so unfair."

* * * * * * * *

COCO

Tita has left. She goes into the sea tonight, I know. She has her fish skin on.

Those are good girls, her friends. I can tell they are kind to animals.

I wonder if they will be in the sea with her?

It is not fair. I want to go, too.

But Tita is right: Miguel would be unhappy if I am not here.

He depends on me to greet him when he gets home.

* * * * * * * *

Jess and Maia walk as quietly as they can, Jess pulling the empty cart. Unfortunately, it rattles. Along the street, curtains part. The girls' journey is not going unwitnessed.

Maia gives an awkward laugh and Jess makes a small wave, indicating, "We're harmless... nothing to see here..."

"Un pueblo pequeño... un infierno grande," Maia

murmurs, trying the adage out.

They're both relieved when they get to the commercial street. "This is the street Tita mentioned, right?"

Maia answers, "I'm pretty sure..." and they look down it, expecting to see the kind of store they both grew up with: a big supermarket with a huge parking lot, open twenty-four hours, shining in the night. Instead, after walking a bit farther, they find a dimly lit place about the size of a U.S. 7-11, and it's closing in ten minutes.

"Good thing we got here in time!" Jess says.

They wheel the cart in and fill it with frozen fish, shrimp, and squid. There's still plenty in the store's small freezer, so Jess asks the owner and he produces a large cardboard box. They empty his freezer of frozen fish, then take the few cans of crab from a shelf and put those in their box, too.

"Let's not forget to buy a can opener!" Maia says.

The owner of the store clearly does not know what to make of these two – what are they? Fifteen? At most eighteen? Buying enough seafood to open a restaurant. But they're friendly and they pay in cash.

He sees they're struggling to balance it all in the cart. He helps them re-load it, and finds two smaller boxes that are easier for Maia to manage carrying.

"Buenas noches," he says, as they head out.

They call back a grateful "Buenas noches," then start to laugh when they're out of earshot.

"I can promise you that we're the first people to buy a Bird's Feast from him!" Jess jokes.

She pushes the cart and Maia carries the boxes down the street. It's a short walk to the spot on the beach where the Pérez boat sits.

They load the boxes into the panga, and Jess says, "One of us should stay here with it..."

Maia looks at Jess, still in her wetsuit. Then she looks down at herself. Her clothes aren't exactly clean – she sits on a guano-coated rock all day, after all – but the front of her is respectable.

"You stay here. I'll go with the cart and one of the boxes."

About an hour later, she returns with another cart-full and the box refilled.

"Needless to say, they thought I was crazy. But they seemed happy to sell their odds and ends. I went to two places. I told them I'd be back tomorrow and they said that was fine."

Jess nods and says, "I guess we're gonna be doing this the next few nights."

They finish loading the boat and Jess says, "Ready?" Maia nods and Jess roars the boat out to sea.

* * * * * * * *

So it's a typical Saturday night in the town. Tourists enjoy dinner out, and locals work to provide it. Tita shepherds vaquitas, Emily plots against vain women half a world away, and Maia and Jess prepare a dinner party for bird couriers. Nothing unusual at all.

PART III: THE PLAN TAKES OFF

It's almost midnight when Maia and Jess approach The Rock.

"Hi, Sammy!" Jess calls to her surfboard sea lion. But he's zonked out on the board and doesn't answer.

They each carry as much up as they can, but a lot of food remains down in the boat. Reaching the top, they take a deep breath and survey the scene. It's a beautiful summer night, with plenty of stars. And there's no barking or screeching; the only sound is the waves hitting the rocks below.

Jess is thinking how peaceful it all is when Maia interrupts with a series of disappointed "tsk" noises.

"What's up?"

"Well, as you can see, the birds have all gone."

"That's not that surprising. We were gone pretty long."

Maia replies, "Yeah, I know. It's just hard to believe we're gonna depend on those…"

"…those friggin' frigatebirds?" jokes Jess.

"Right," Maia laughs. The she checks the sky again: not a single bird in sight. "Jess, you start laying the table… while I try to get the dinner guests to show up…"

Jess scrambles down to the panga to finish unloading it.

Above, Maia starts shrieking. It's the call she first used to lure them: the sound of a female frigatebird.

Nothing happens.

Maia tries again, louder.

Again nothing happens.

Though Jess is far below, she can tell by the ongoing shrieks that Maia is frustrated.

Jess climbs to the top and starts dropping seafood onto the ground when Maia mutters, "Oh, God, I guess I'll have to get Mrs. B involved..." Jess just keeps on task, opening bags and cans, spreading out the contents, and waiting to see what happens.

Maia has the phone in her hand, hesitating. Jess realizes she's hoping the food alone will draw the birds in. But no one comes, so finally Maia makes the call. After some introductory squawks about being awakened, Mrs. Bixby starts to shriek like a female frigatebird.

And again nothing happens. Clearly, the birds aren't interested.

Jess looks up from her seafood buffet and says, "Well, I guess 'trustworthy' definitely doesn't describe them..."

Maia nods in disgust and resumes conversing with Mrs. Bixby. After a few moments, her look of annoyance has turned into one of defiance. She shuts the phone off and commences to make a series of shrieks and screeches.

Slowly but surely, the birds return.

Jess, opening the final bag of shrimp, asks, "How did you get them back? What did you say to them?"

"I said, 'Seems to me Magnificent Frigatebird is going to be changed to Lying-No-good-Cowardly-Bird any minute now.'"

* * * * * * * *

The frigatebirds show no signs of embarrassment. They're too busy eating. The hope is they would gorge themselves, and gorging is what they're doing. They've never seen such an array of tasty food.

Jess eyes them doubtfully, "Are we really going to rely on

135

them to do this? Not only make the journey, but deliver the solution and get it into bladders?"

Maia says, "Oh, they'll do it, alright."

Jess is skeptical. "I believe in what we learned at camp. You know I do. That we're all one. But do you see them?" she gestures to the birds, who continue feasting. "Do you see them tearing into that slop, without a care in the world? They seem pretty sure what's important: looking out for number one!"

Maia turns and looks at her. "You have to have faith, Jess. You know that." She pauses, then smiles and says, "Besides, Mrs. Bixby knows three of their mothers."

* * * * * * * *

For the first night in a long time, Tita simply enjoys her patrol. She feels confident in Emily's plan.

While Tita swims, and Jess and Maia feed frigatebirds in the starlight, Emily communicates with the bodhis in China by video conference call.

Mei Li usually spends her time as a Panda Protector. She has just left a misty forest in Sichuan Province, where she was a surrogate mother for an orphaned cub. Since the baby's grown, and they're making some headway on panda conservation, she's got time to help with the Baja project. She's still getting used to sleeping in a bed after months of sleeping in trees.

"I have the names, addresses, phone numbers, and shopping habits of the twenty biggest customers for totoaba bladder in Guangzhou," she says.

"And I have the same kind of information for Hong Kong," says Lynn Chang. Lynn volunteered for this mission. She has ties to the work: her family led efforts to save the Yangtze river porpoise. Sadly, in 2006, the river porpoise was declared extinct. Every morning, Lynn starts her day by chanting "Never Again" in forty different bird languages.

Emily says, "Strong work, ladies. That'll help when we get the solution over there. In the meantime, while I'm waiting for the supplies to come, I thought we could begin getting our stories out there."

"Make up cases?" Lynn asks.

"Exactly. Why wait for the real thing, when we can make them up?" Emily asks. "The problem is that I don't speak much Chinese – just a little Mandarin, and no Cantonese – and I don't have access to the search engines there."

"No problem," Lynn replies. "I have contacts at Baidu. They'll help me get the cases to the top of the results..." Baidu is the Chinese equivalent of Google.

"And I'll do case reports in English for any Chinese-American customers," Emily says. "Get those rumors started: 'You can't trust that fish bladder from Mexico'..."

* * * * * * * *

On Sunday, the Pérez family allows itself a lie-in. They get up at the unheard-of hour of 9:00 a.m.

Miguel says, "Well, Tita, I was thinking about what we could do today... it would be nice if your mother could have some time to herself. What do you say to taking the boat out?"

Tita nearly chokes on her sweet roll. "Oh, Papá, um..."

"It's been so long since we did that."

She hates disappointing him. Panicked, she looks around the kitchen, her eyes spotting a cactus outside the window. "I was hoping we'd go to el Valle de los Gigantes and see the cacti."

"In this heat?" he asks her incredulously. They all have a tolerance for heat, but Tita isn't fond of it.

"It's not so bad... we could take a picnic."

"A desert picnic? That's what my Tita wants?"

Tita nods.

"A desert picnic it is."

* * * * * * * *

Sunday comes and goes, with Tita and Miguel in the

desert, María reading a book in the shade, Coco sleeping in the sun. Jess, Maia, and Maia's birds patrol the Area. Emily tries to focus on her Internet rumor-mongering.

That night, Jess and Maia do their second night of seafood buying. The store owner apologizes – they emptied him out last night – but promises he'll have more tomorrow. They buy some fruit for themselves and tell him they'll be back the next evening.

Maia and Jess hit the restaurants, then ferry loads of seafood out to The Rock. The birds fly in, as if to the feast born. They should always eat like this!

When Monday morning arrives, Emily can barely contain her excitement. It's time to get started!

* * * * * * * *

The cab driver doesn't know what to think when the lanky teenager bounds out of the apartment building and says, yes, I'm the one who called for a ride to the airstrip.

He's on the receiving end of a lecture in Spanish about the cacti of his homeland, when they arrive at the small airport.

"I'll just be a few minutes," she says.

He nods and turns to his newspaper, eager to read about his football club in peace.

He waits and waits and begins to worry he's been the victim of a prank when the girl approaches his car. "There's more boxes than I expected," she says. "I'll need your help – I'll pay, of course."

He doesn't mind. It's good to stretch his legs. He gets out of the car and enters the building. The customs agent reviews the paperwork and says, "Everything's in order... It's these seven boxes."

Seven boxes, some labelled "Infectious" and some just "For Medical Use." The driver's body language tells Emily he doesn't want to get too close to some of them.

"It's ok, I'll take those!" She has him take the ones without the red warning label.

Just as they've finished loading the taxi and are about to head off she cries, "Wait!" She hurriedly scans the boxes and announces, "There's got to be one more!" She runs inside, and emerges ten minutes later, carrying an eighth box, the biggest of them all.

"We have a lot of this in our yard." Excited, she's reverted to English... but in any language, it only makes sense to her.

He gives her a look that clearly says, "What is all this?"

She just smiles innocently at him and says, back in Spanish, "It's for my science project."

* * * * * * * *

Once she's back at the apartment, Emily unpacks everything – except that huge carton forwarded from home. "Gotta be careful with that!"

She organizes her supplies, placing the viral cultures in the freezer. That should keep their growth in check and reduce the risk of contaminating the kitchen surfaces.

When her workplace is orderly and it's all finally to her satisfaction, she opens the refrigerator, and removes the two totoaba bladders she got from the marine sanctuary.

Emily puts the butterscotch yellow bladders on the counter. She bends her head and says in benediction, "May the deaths of these fish not have been in vain. Bless the work I will do."

Then she carves one of the bladders up into ten pieces, and returns the other, whole, to the refrigerator.

She spends the day using various strengths of virus solution and stabilizers on the ten segments. She takes detailed notes of each test on her laptop.

After many hours of work, all but one sample has turned brownish green. "That's not going to sell very well," she mumbles with dissatisfaction. Still, the one sample looks promising.

* * * * * * * *

While Emily's doing virology, Tita and Maia and Jess are going about their business: restaurant work and vaquita patrols.

They haven't seen Emily since the big Conference at The Rock, but they feel confident she's solved the totoaba problem.

"The solution is the wart solution!" Maia laughs to Jess as they finish their patrol.

Jess laughs, and asks, "Ready?" Then they leap off The Rock and fly to town to start their evening purchasing rounds.

Once at the small grocery store, Jess chats with the owner as she pays. She notices a drawing on the wall behind him and gestures to it. "Look, Maia!"

Her friend peers at it and smiles, asking, "Vaquita?"

The owner smiles back and says, "Sí, mi hijo." Jess explains to Maia, "He says his son drew it." To the owner, she says, "Señor, I'm Jess... and this is Maia."

"I'm Rafael Díaz," he replies.

"Nice to meet you. Please tell your son we like vaquitas, too."

* * * * * * * *

When they get to The Rock (this time in the panga), they're in such high spirits that it's even a pleasure to see the gluttonous frigatebirds come for their feast.

"Hey, Fairbanks!" Jess calls to the leader, who looks up from the clam he's pulling from its shell.

"Looking good... putting on some weight!" adds Maia.

The bird returns to its meal, fluffing his feathers as if to say, "Of course I'm looking good."

* * * * * * * *

On her laptop, Emily checks the data of the promising sample. "I used Flask #8 on it."

She removes the remaining intact bladder from the refrigerator. She cuts this in half, and puts half back.

She takes a tiny syringe and injects Flask #8 liquid into

twenty places on the half-bladder, then uses a gloved finger to smear the liquid over the bladder's surface.

"I have to get some sleep. I'll see how it is in the morning."

She leaves the treated half on the counter and goes to bed.

At dawn, though she promised herself to wait and eat breakfast first, her patience gives out. Besides, it's right there: the half-bladder on the counter.

Brownish green.

"Argh... this isn't going well."

Back to it. Another day in the lab. In the back of her mind, she worries: will she need more bladders?

As if drawn to a treasure at a museum, she opens the refrigerator and stares at the remaining untreated half-bladder. Such a small piece, such a small amount of tissue.

"I hope it'll be enough," she says, heading back to work at the counter. She doesn't even notice skipping breakfast.

* * * * * * * *

TONY BAI

The Idealist is proving to be more of a problem than I expected. My informants tell me we absolutely cannot buy him off. He's an Eagle Scout, this guy.

He has two children but they're young. And Mr. Responsible is setting aside some of his pathetic monthly pay in a college fund, so that's not a pressing issue.

As far as their medical situation goes, they're fine healthy children. That's obvious in his desk photo, which was scanned to me.

Looks like even their teeth will come in straight. No big orthodontic bills to squeeze the family budget.

So... I started to talk about possible accidents. Nothing fatal... for now. Just enough to keep him out of commission for a while.

But they think he'll take a vacation soon. That would be easier. And safer.

But we'll do what we have to do.

* * * * * * * *

Tita is shaken as she emerges from the water that night. She encountered two gillnets. "It's been weeks since there were nets in the Refuge!" The poachers are back out.

She sleeps poorly that night and muddles her way through the breakfast shift. María can tell she's worried about something.

"What is it, Tita?"

"There were nets last night, Mamá. It's been a long time since I saw any in the Refuge."

María can see she's hesitating, wanting to ask something. María rescues her by saying, "Skip lunch. I'll manage. Go see the team."

Tita nods, smiling gratefully at her mother.

It's a fiercely hot day and the beach is crowded. Tita walks far up the coast to find a safe place, then she enters the water. Once she feels she's past any observation, she stops her surface freestyle swimming and dives deep, torpedoing to The Rock.

Sammy is hanging out, as usual, on Jess's surfboard.

"Emily was right: you will miss that when they go," Tita thinks.

But he reads her thoughts, and barks unhappily at her.

Finishing her scramble to the top, she calls out, "Hello!"

"Hello, stranger!" Maia hugs her. "What's up?"

"I need some bird help."

The girls sit down and Tita explains, "There are nets again in the Refuge."

Maia looks alarmed. "The pelicans didn't report anything..."

"It's not their fault. The Refuge is big."

Maia mulls it over. She asks, "Nets are illegal there, right?"

Tita nods.

"So it's not just a matter of keeping our vaqs safe... if we find out who placed the nets, we know who our problem is."

Tita feels herself tense up. She's been avoiding thinking about this. Does she really want to know if some of her neighbors are murderers? She replies wearily, "Yes, that's right."

"Let me get Cornelius in on this one."

Maia stands up and lifts her head to the sky. Then she lets out a series of cries exactly mimicking a seagull.

"That's very good!" Tita exclaims.

Maia looks at her and smiles. "I've improved a lot, if I do say so myself."

Several yellow-footed gulls start to approach but Maia cries again, pointing to the largest one. The others turn and head back over the sea.

Cornelius swoops in, landing gracefully a few feet from Maia. He cocks his head at her, then turns to Tita and does the same. His version of hello.

Maia and Cornelius speak for a moment, then Maia turns to Tita and says, "Cornelius will personally – I mean, birdly – cover that region tonight."

Cornelius squawks and Maia translates: "He can do two things if he sees the poachers: he can either swoop in and get a piece of skin or hair, and we can use that for tracking..."

Tita briefly wonders, "Would Coco be up for tracking?" She isn't sure he'd be able to do it. He's a smart dog but they've never used him for something like that.

Maia continues: "Or he can drop one of his feathers into the boat and we can retrieve it later, and figure out who owns the boat."

Tita appreciates the bird's ideas, but she knows what has to happen. She says, "Tell Cornelius he should watch from the sky. If he sees the boat, he must call to me and I will swim in. I will identify it."

Searching Tita's face, Maia says, "That's dangerous, Tita."

"I know. But it's the only way."

* * * * * * * *

Maia works with Cornelius and Tita for about the next hour. Gradually, with Cornelius flying farther and farther away, Tita learns to pick out his call from among the many gulls. She learns his cries for, "I see them. Come here" and "Not here. Follow me to another section."

Their exercises complete, Tita and Cornelius agree to meet in the Refuge that night. Then Cornelius salutes the girls and flies off. Tita's just about to leave when they hear Sammy barking and Jess saying a quick hello in return. She sounds agitated.

"Maia," she calls as she finishes climbing up the rockface. "Oh, Tita, hi," she says, pleased but surprised to see her there. "Girls, it was awful. I came back because I needed a break."

Maia and Tita just wait as Jess gulps some water.

"It's ok, in the end. But one of the Eight was caught in a net. Three of the others came in to help me dislodge her. The poor thing was choking when she got to the surface."

Tita shakes her head. "It's terrible to see."

"I hope she'll be ok... poor Number 7... I think she's one of the older ones... I hope it didn't frighten her to death." She adds, "I can't bear to give them names. If I did, I would never leave Baja... well, Tita, what brings you here?"

They explain the situation and Jess asks, "Do you want me to go with you tonight?" She doesn't say it but Tita knows she's asking, "Will you be ok if it's someone you know?"

Tita answers, "Thank you, Yess" – she smiles at her own struggle with the "J" sound – "but no. I can do it. You need your rest."

* * * * * * * *

Tita can tell the vaquitas are on edge. She told some of them about the nets and now they all know. Plus, they've probably heard about the close call for Number 7 in the Area. They're in slightly bigger groups tonight. El Jefe encouraged this, and told them to scream if they get into trouble.

"All will be ok," she says as she swims by the vaquitas in the southwestern corner of the Refuge. This is where the nets were last night, and where Cornelius and she agreed to start.

Tita swims anxiously around. Thank goodness her wrist isn't glowing. All she needs is for that to give her away to the poachers.

El Sud comes and swims with her. At first Tita thinks he just wants to give her company, but slowly she realizes he knows it's a mission. She has mixed feelings about this: she wants the vaquitas to enjoy their lives and leave the work and worrying to her. But El Sud is staying put right by her.

They move together, Sud surfacing every two or three minutes to breathe, and Tita joining to listen for Cornelius. She hears the gull crying out, "Not here, not here."

Underwater, Tita keeps her eyes peeled, as ever, for nets. But there's more urgency, now that she knows one is or was nearby. She doesn't want to find herself in one, with the poachers retrieving it and finding a human catch.

Up and down, up and down. Up to the surface to listen for Cornelius, down into the water to look for nets. It's nerve-wracking.

Hours go by but she's lost track of time. She's also lost track of where she is in the Refuge. So much of it is just open water, with few geographical landmarks.

Up and down, up and down. Loyal Sud by her side.

Up again. This time... is it? The cry that means there's a boat?

She stops and listens. Sud can sense something important happening and he remains motionless beside her, his snout shining in the dim moonlight.

"I see them! Come here! I see them! Come here!" shrieks the gull. It's very faint, off a bit to the south.

Tita and Sud dive under and swim in that direction.

"Come here!" the bird's shrieks are louder.

They swim some more.

"Here!" louder still.

A few more lengths of swimming, then Tita surfaces. This time she can see the panga. It's white, but to her mind, it's the same dark boat she saw the night of Lola's death. Enraged, she feels she could overturn it and drown the men.

Shaking, she dips her head underwater. El Sud's face is right next to hers. She tells him, "Sudi, stay back. It's a boat... that means they have nets. Stay back!"

Sud nods and doesn't go with her as she swims in to get closer to the boat.

It's difficult gauging when to come up. The water is dark and disorienting. Just how far away is the panga? She must be careful not to show herself. But she also has to get close enough to see the boat and see the poachers.

She paddles the water equivalent of baby steps, then lets just one ear come above the water.

The gull continues his mad cries. He can't see Tita and so he keeps calling for her.

More tiny movements, more tiny breaks in the plane of the water, as her ear tries to hear anything besides Cornelius.

One of the fishermen yells, "That damn bird!" Tita can just hear the man. Is it a familiar voice? Tita thinks it might be, but is she just projecting that?

"Here! Here!" Cornelius shrieks.

Tita calms herself and says to the gull telepathically, "It's ok, Cornelius, I'm here."

The gull stops crying, but continues his wheeling motions above the boat. Tita lifts her head ever so slightly, and can see three men. She can't make out any details, and so she swims even closer.

She surfaces as gently as she ever has, and then realizes she's overshot the mark. She's within a few yards of the boat, in real danger of their seeing her.

Luckily Cornelius has spotted her, and he starts wailing,

distracting the men. He swoops in, still in safety above them, but close enough that they're worried he's going to attack. They start waving oars to fend him off. He's shrieking and somersaulting above their heads.

As they're busy fighting Cornelius off, Tita gets a good look.

Two are strangers. The third one she knows.

* * * * * * * *

EL SUD

Anita returns to me. She comes away from the evil ones and tells me to wait with her.

We are at the surface and watch. There are three humans on a raft. Two are standing up, pulling at the netzz in our sea. Many small fish are trapped. It's horrible.

The tallest man stands up, helping to pull the netzz on to the raft. Something heavy makes this hard. Finally, he and the other men get all the netzz in. They raise the heavy thing high. It's a young hammerhead shark.

They don't like him, and he gets dumped back into the sea. He will swim another day.

The men did not find what they were looking for.

Us.

* * * * * * * *

Tita sees Cornelius circling above, waiting for her.

She turns to say goodbye to Sud. "Thanks for being here. I'm sorry you had to see that, Sudi. But now you know what we're up against."

He looks at her, listening. Then he emits a long series of short clicks.

Tita floats gently and lets the sounds come over her. Slowly, she realizes he's confused.

"No, Sudi. It's not the vaquita that the humans want. It's the totoaba."

Anyone could understand his next noises: buzzes and clicks of shocked disbelief.

Tita laughs. "I agree! You're much more charming – and much better-looking than the totoaba! And much more intelligent! But not all humans are so intelligent... and they want the totoaba for some pretty stupid reasons."

Sud just shakes his snout. What a problem these humans can be.

"Goodbye, Sudi," Tita says, putting her arm around his body. He nuzzles her and then they part ways.

Tita zooms back to the beach, but she's no match for Cornelius's flying. He's on the sand waiting for her when she emerges.

"Well, Cornelius, what are we going to do about Fernando Vega?"

* * * * * * * *

Tita can't speak much Gull but the bird understands her and knows his task. After a brief discussion, they part ways, the gull saluting her as always. Flying, he'll quickly find his subject again.

Tita walks home, drained.

She's never had an opinion one way or another about Fernando Vega. He occasionally fished with her father, and he occasionally comes to her mother's restaurant. If asked, she would've guessed that he wasn't the smartest – he never had a fishing crew of his own. Well, not a legal one, anyway. And she'd probably say – though none of the fishermen she knows is rich! – that he was one of the poorer ones.

She sees him in her mind's eye, and realizes for the first

time how stooped his posture is, as if life's beaten him down. In a way, her heart goes out to him. Though she loves her vaquitas fiercely, she understands that it's not easy making a living here.

And she understands that she's growing up, and that there aren't always easy answers.

But what's done is done, and though she has empathy for him, there's nothing she can do. He's about to be tracked by a stubborn seagull.

* * * * * * * *

The next day, Tita is so tired her eyes can barely stay open. The bright morning sun isn't helping: her squinting quickly leads to her eyes shutting completely. How lovely it would be to fall asleep against the counter. Just for a few minutes...

"Tita... Tita! Wake up, it's me Emily!"

Tita shakes her head to clear away the sleep, then asks, "How are you? Do you want breakfast?"

"Could I have some toast? I'm not doing so great, I have to tell you."

Tita looks at her with concern. Emily was so confident. But today she looks defeated.

A tourist couple comes in, and Tita gestures for Emily to take a seat on the patio for them to talk when Tita gets a free moment.

Tita takes the orders for the couple and is about to head back to the kitchen when she sees someone out on the malecón: Fernando Vega. And he's walking straight towards her.

Her heart jumps: does he know she saw him last night?

"Don't be silly, Tita," she tells herself, then notices Cornelius behind him. The gull stays outside on the sidewalk as the man enters the patio.

She brings the orders to her mother then heads back to the customers. She gathers her courage and approaches him as he picks a table.

"Buenos días, Sr. Vega," she says, hoping it sounds friendly.

He's always been a man of few words, and there's not much to tell from his, "Buenos días." It seems normal enough.

Nervously, she puts a menu in front of him, asking if he'd like coffee.

"Sí," he says looking at the menu. Tita steals a look at him. He looks even more tired than she does. Like he had a rough night.

Cornelius remains on the sidewalk, pretending to be interested in a patch of gravel.

Tita takes the toast to Emily, who says a little loudly, "Can we talk now?"

Tita widens her eyes and tilts her head, trying to express, "Shhh... that man there can't be trusted."

Emily is slow on the uptake, "What? What's the issue?... oh, oh, yes. Well it's ok if you don't have cranberry juice. Orange juice will be fine."

It doesn't take long for the restaurant to clear out. The couple's in a hurry to get on with sightseeing, and Sr. Vega's not a man to linger over food. He pays Tita, thanks her in a distracted way, and leaves. Cornelius watches him pass by, then flies and follows him at a distance.

"What was that about?" Emily asks after he's gone.

"He's one of the poachers... Cornelius and I identified him last night."

"Do you know him?!"

"Only a little... What's going on with you?"

"Oh, Tita, it isn't going well at all. And I've used up almost all the bladder tissue. I just have one-sixteenth left. Everything keeps turning a gross color. There's no way we can put it up for sale."

Hearing this upsets Tita, but she hides it for her friend's sake. She says, "It will work. Don't be sad."

Emily offers, "Look on the bright side?"

Tita looks confused.

"'Look on the bright side' – it means to see the good, to be positive."

"Yes! Let's 'be positive' – the sun is shining, it's many weeks since a vaquita died..."

"And we have a bird ally tracking our man!"

The two just look at each other and start laughing.

* * * * * * *

Emily heads home, channeling Tita's positivity. She talks through the reactions that might be causing the discoloration. She does this out loud (and more than one person avoids her on the sidewalk.) By the time she's back at the apartment, she has decided on a strategy.

"Here goes nothing," she jokes, taking the final sixteenth of bladder out of the refrigerator.

She cuts this in two, making impossibly small segments. She returns one of them to the refrigerator.

She tweaks the latest solution slightly and, as before, uses a micro-syringe to inject small amounts throughout the segment, then coats it.

"And now we wait."

* * * * * * *

Tita is distracted as she and María serve lunch. If Emily's plan doesn't work, what will they do?

She's thought before that the vaquitas need more allies. Friends who can help them, by patrolling for nets or spreading word among them. Friends who don't have to work, or go to school.

"I'll talk to El Jefe about Mateo," she decides.

* * * * * * *

It's 8:00 p.m. Emily can't take it any longer. It's been nine hours, but she feels it's been weeks.

"The moment of truth!" she says, approaching the

151

counter, but keeping her eyes closed.

"One... two... three..." she opens her eyes. It takes a split second to register the sight: the bladder segment is unchanged. Same butterscotch yellow.

"Yes!" she cries triumphantly. No discoloration!

Not even really knowing what she's doing, she grabs her keys and races out of the apartment.

* * * * * * * *

COCO

The nervous one is outside. I will go get Tita.

I really like this creature. But she thinks too much.

* * * * * * * *

"Tita, it worked! I had to come tell you!" Emily whisper-shouts this, trying but failing to keep her joy quiet.

Tita feels relief flooding in.

"Thank you for telling me, Emily. Thank you!"

The two stand giggling and smiling at each other, with Coco a silent witness.

Tita has to go back inside. But before she does she says, "It will be a happy patrol tonight."

"Give those vaquitas my best!" Emily says, and heads off. She's so elated she just keeps walking, and ends up on the beach.

Standing on the shore, she lets the summer evening embrace her. She looks up, and the stars seem to smile back. For once, her brain is quiet, the only thought being: "I did it!"

With her gaze heavenwards, she doesn't see the white panga on the horizon, heading out to sea, with Cornelius flying above it.

* * * * * * * *

Even though The Rock surface is... rocky... Jess and Maia are sleeping soundly. It takes Cornelius a full minute to wake them up, with gradually louder shrieks.

"Whoa, whoa, what?" Maia wakes. "What?!" She opens her lids and sees the gull's bead eyes three inches from her own.

"Cornelius, what's going on?"

Jess sits up. "Hey, Cornelius. Thanks for the morning alarm... oh, it's not morning," she looks out, seeing the night sky.

"Squawk, shriek, squawk!"

"Jess, we gotta go. Cornelius has tracked poachers into the Area. And they've trapped a vaquita."

The girls stand up and leap into the air, catching an updraft. Following Cornelius, they're at the Area in three minutes. In the moonlight, they see a panga to the east. Someone is using a flashlight, looking over the contents of the vessel.

Jess and Maia circle overhead, looking like enormous hawks. Maia asks, "What should we do? If we sweep in to get the vaq, we'll blow our cover."

Jess says, "Yes, it's too bad, but I don't see a choice. We can't let the vaquita die."

Maia nods, and they fly closer. With a look at one another, they're just about to dive-bomb the boat, when a strange thing happens: they hear muffled noises, what sounds like an argument.

The girls circle a bit closer trying to hear what they say. Even Cornelius is silent.

No words reach them, but they see some quick movements, and the flash of light on steel. The panga lists to one side as the tallest man pushes something out of the boat. It enters the sea with a faint splash.

Flying higher, Maia and Jess see a porpoise surface fifty feet from the boat. His blowhole snuffles for breath, but he's free.

Then the man lifts something slightly smaller. Casually,

using the same knife that freed the vaquita, he slits the quivering totoaba. He cuts the bladder out, and pushes the rest of the fish out of the boat.

Without speaking, Maia and Jess coordinate their efforts. Jess flies farther away to dive unnoticed into the sea, then races underwater up to the boat. Maia flies closer in, to support Jess if she needs it.

Jess hears the tall man say, "There. Our third totoaba of the night. I am not here to kill vaquitas."

The other two just grumble, ashamed of themselves.

"It took no time to let that animal go. We have three bladders... it's been a good night."

Jess ducks back under the water and heads off, finding the vaquita. She knows him as Number 5. "You'll be ok," she murmurs, hugging him. She feels him shaking, fear and relief filling his body. "Go now and rest... we're here tonight and there won't be any more problems."

Far from the boat, Jess surfaces, and Maia comes to hover above. She says, "Thank goodness he let the vaquita go. But what was all that about?" Maia didn't understand the Spanish.

Jess explains what she heard just as Cornelius flies over to join the girls.

"Maia, ask Cornelius which man he's been following."

Maia squawks, then Cornelius squawks back. Nodding, Maia says, "It's the same one, Jess. The tall, stooped man."

"Keep following him, Cornelius! Let's find out what they do with those bladders."

* * * * * * * *

CORNELIUS

These are humans I can work with, these girls.

I follow this man so easily. He doesn't even know it. The night helps, of course. But when he passes a streetlight and I start to worry he's suspecting something, I fly to a pole and look

dumb. We birds can look very dumb, when it suits us.
This guy isn't such a bad guy. I saw him release that vaquita.

But he's bad enough.

My brother Horatio was killed in one of their nets. If I told
him once, I told him a hundred times: stay away from the piles
of fish in the sea. Piles of fish aren't natural. Horatio knew this.
He was no fool. But he was a little bit lazy and a little bit cocky,
and there was all that glorious food just sitting there. So he
flew on down to have a feast, and then the net closed in.

I can still hear Horatio screeching. I can still see the net being
lifted and taken away. I followed it as far as I could but when
they took it inside a building near the docks, I couldn't follow.
Besides, by then his screeches were silent.

I almost feel sorry for this man. He looks haunted. His
shoulders droop. He's never flown in his life. In so many ways,
I have it better than him.

Is that why the humans hurt us? Because they're jealous?

But these girls... I trust them. I can work with them.

* * * * * * * *

Emily's nighttime reverie on the beach doesn't last long.
"Back to work!" she commands herself. "I have to make the
solution for the birds to take!"

She returns to the apartment and puts on a pot of coffee.
She can almost hear her mother's disapproval: "Sixteen year
olds should not drink coffee!"

"Sorry, Mom," she says, lifting her mug in salute. "But I
have a long night ahead of me."

As Cornelius tracks Fernando, Emily launches into
production mode.

155

By 3:00 a.m., the viral component is done.

"Now for the Pennsylvania Pride," she says. She goes into the bedroom and gets a long sleeved cotton shirt and puts it on over her T shirt.

"Gotta be careful." She opens that big carton.

At 5:30 a.m., her work is completed. With a satisfied smile, she sets her alarm and lies down. "Just a quick nap... then I'll get in touch with the team."

* * * * * * * *

Jess gets to the restaurant early. She's sitting on the sidewalk when María and Tita arrive. María unlocks the door. "I can get started, Tita. You talk with Jess."

Jess is just about to launch in, when they hear Emily calling at the door, "Tita? Sra. Pérez?"

"Come on in, Emily!" Jess replies. "I'm here, too."

The three girls settle at a table. Jess begins, "So, last night, Cornelius came and woke me and Maia: the poachers were in the Area. And a vaquita was trapped!"

Tita and Emily are about to get really upset when Jess spares them and says, "Don't worry, Number 5 is ok. Believe it or not, the poacher..."

"Was he tall? And...?" Tita hangs her head and hunches her back a bit.

"Yes, that's him."

Tita nods, "Sr. Vega. Fernando Vega."

"Well, Fernando isn't all bad – he let the vaquita go!"

Tita can barely believe it. She says a silent thank you. Emily catches her eye and gives a look that says, "Who knew? Maybe there's some decency after all."

"Yeah, he said he wasn't there to kill vaquitas, and they already got three bladders..."

Emily interrupts, "Three bladders?"

"Yep."

"Do you know where they are?"

"Cornelius is looking into that right now."

They look at Emily expectantly. Why is she so interested in the bladders?

Emily explains, "I have some great news, which Tita already knows. My experiments yesterday worked! But I'm almost out of tissue. If I could get those bladders and run more tests, I'd feel much more confident. Before asking those frigatebirds to fly seven thousand miles..."

Jess listens. Without looking at either of them, she says to the air in front of her, "So you want to steal three totoaba bladders?"

Emily squirms in her chair, "Not to put too fine a point on it... but, yes."

Jess turns and gives her a mischievous smile.

* * * * * * * *

María makes breakfast for the girls, which they eat with relish. Things are looking up! The wart solution is stable in the bladders, Fernando's not all bad, and Number 5 was saved!

When they've finished, Jess stands up and says, "Let's give María her restaurant back. It's probably best that we not all be seen together too often. I'll swim out to The Rock and wait for Cornelius there."

"And I'll go home and dole out solution. For the birds to carry, and for testing if we get those bladders."

Tita stands up and says, "And I'll help Mamá!"

The three laugh, feeling optimistic. Emily's the first to leave, Jess telling her, "We'll get word to you when we know about the bladders."

* * * * * * * *

María and Tita help Jess load up her waterproof backpack with some provisions, then Jess heads to the beach. It's early on a weekday, so no one sees her dive under. She blasts out to The Rock.

"Hey, Sammy," she says, as she climbs the facade. The sea

lion barks a sleepy hello from his surfboard perch. It does her heart good to see him fat and happy.

Jess finds Maia tired but awake. "Good morning. I brought you some breakfast. I thought you could use some energy, after the night we had."

"Thanks. I'm just sitting waiting for Cornelius."

"That's why I'm here, too. By the way, I learned our villain-hero's name: Fernando."

Fernando. Hmm. Maia doesn't know whether to be mad or grateful. She takes the food and eats while Jess lies down and stares at the sky. Occasionally a brown pelican flies in to give the word: nothing suspicious in the Refuge.

* * * * * * * *

The day is getting to be very hot, and Jess and Maia are starting to doze off, when Cornelius arrives. Again, the bird has to screech them awake, but this time it only takes one call.

Jess watches as Maia and the gull discuss where he's been and what he's seen. After several minutes, Maia turns to Jess and says, "Cornelius followed the panga. When they landed, Fernando paid the other two. They left, and Fernando took the bladders to a warehouse on the docks. It sounds like there was a combination lock – Cornelius said, 'He spun a little wheel and the door opened.' Anyway, Vega put the bladders in there. Cornelius knows where it is... he can show us."

Jess says, "Ok, great. Let's go get them."

Maia raises a good point: "How are we going to get inside? Break in?"

Jess doesn't answer at first. She doesn't like the idea of damaging property, or worse, leaving a trail. But whoever's involved... well, they're going to find out something happened when the bladders are gone, aren't they?

After mulling it over, she says, "Let's call Emily and see what she thinks."

* * * * * * * *

Emily just finished separating the solution into thirty vials. Now she's considering the overall situation. If she gets more bladders – if Cornelius traces them successfully – she has just enough materials for the extra testing. But no more than that.

"I should order more supplies, and make more solution... just in case. Also, some tinier tubes would be better for the birds than these 3 ml kind," she says aloud, scratching her right wrist absent-mindedly.

She looks at the counter. There sits the final one thirty-second piece, which she injected about an hour ago, when she got home from the restaurant. It still looks like plain old totoaba bladder. Next to it sits the successful piece from yesterday, also unchanged.

Musing over these, and scratching her wrist, she thinks about the order: she'll need more virus, some mini tubes... and it would be great to track the birds, so better get one or two satellite GPS transmitters. And... here's an idea: a special piece of equipment... expensive, but worth it. Best to cover their tracks.

She's just about to call The Agency when her phone rings. It's Jess.

"Hey, there. What's going on?"

Emily listens as Jess explains: they want to steal bladders from the warehouse. Does she know how to pick a padlock? If not, she and Maia will break in.

"A standard combination padlock? Yes, that's no problem." She listens for another moment and then interjects, "I don't think today would be good. You see, I think we've got to replace the bladders so they don't know we're onto them.

"Yes, replace them... with dummies." She listens for a moment and then says, "I'll explain later. But if you and Maia want to help me... well, hopefully, the Agency can get the supplies to me in a day or two... and then we can make the casts."

They end the call and Emily starts to make one more. Just as she's about to press the number, she says, "I'd better look up which filament color to get!"

She turns to her laptop and does a quick color search. Maybe too quick.

Then she calls the Agency. "Hello? It's Emily again, in Baja. Listen, I'm going to need some more things, ASAP. Micro-syringes and micro-pipettes. Also, some 2 ml tubes with snap closures. And more HPV cultures... And two satellite transmitters... the frigatebirds each weigh about fifty ounces, so they could carry a twenty-two gram device."

She hesitates, realizing it's starting to get expensive. She gulps, then says authoritatively, "And a 3D printer, with #17 yellow filament."

* * * * * * * *

It's an uneventful Saturday. Since The Agency told her the supplies won't come until tomorrow, Emily is out of work for the moment, and sleeps in. Tita and her mother have a normal day at the restaurant. Maia and Jess patrol the Area without incident.

At night, Tita enjoys her patrol, rejecting the idea of introducing El Jefe to Mateo. It would just stress him, and Emily's plan looks like it will work.

Maia and Jess throw another feast for the frigatebirds, who've become enormous right before their eyes.

Just another uneventful Saturday. Tourists swim and fish, and The Bodhi Sisters go about their business.

* * * * * * * *

There's not a lot of cab business on a Sunday morning, so the taxi driver's grateful for the fare. Grateful and surprised. He recognizes the address when he gets the call. Can it really be the same client? The teenager again? Yes, here she comes, striding out.

"Hola," she says cheerily.

"El aeropuerto?" he asks.

"Sí, el aeropuerto."

"Más por tu proyecto?" (More for your project?)

"Sí!" she says heartily.

It's not a long ride and it seems even shorter today. "I'll just be a moment," she says when they get there. He nods and turns to his newspaper, checking on his football club.

After about fifteen minutes she emerges balancing a tower of small boxes on top of a large one. "Señor, there's one more box. It's very big. Can you help me? No red label, I promise!"

"Of course." He likes this thin crazy girl. He goes into the terminal and gets the box containing the 3D printer. Little does he know that the contents cost more than two months' salary.

When they arrive back at the apartment, the cabdriver helps her bring the things into the small lobby. Before she even has a chance to take it, she notices that he even carries in one of the red viral boxes.

"Muchas gracias," she says, handing him the fare and a very large tip. "The Agency thanks you, too!"

* * * * * * * *

Jess and Maia arrive at Emily's and the three settle into work. All they have to guide them color-wise are the two tiny segments of bladder lying on the counter.

"G, those little bits of fish rind are not giving me a sense of what we're going for," Maia complains.

"Ah! Let me get the photos! I took some when I got the bladders from the sanctuary," Emily goes into the bedroom and retrieves some paper prints.

"Is the color accurate?" Jess asks, looking at the paper. "Did you have enough ink in the printer?"

Emily peers at the photos and says, "That's right on, I'd say."

"Then this plastic is not the right shade," Jess says, holding up the spool of filament.

Maia agrees, "Yeah, it's beige instead of yellow. G, what do you think would help get it right?"

Emily is now only half-listening, as she's hooking up the

161

computer to the 3D printer and thinking of how the shapes will turn out. "Thank goodness I took those photos... and from lots of angles!"

"G? What can we do to get the right color?" Maia asks again.

Emily turns from the computer and faces her friends, stating, "Well, we could concentrate the urobilin from our urine and use it as a dye."

"That's seriously gross, G," protests Maia.

Emily, realizing she's alone on this, says, "Well, yellow food coloring would probably do the trick."

It's clear that Emily has to be the one to set up the printer. The other two have no idea how it works. So Jess says to Maia, "Why don't we go see our friend Rafael Díaz?"

"Won't he be surprised we're not buying fish for once!"

* * * * * * * *

"Hola, Sr. Díaz."

He gives the girls a wide smile. Jess translates for Maia that he says, "You're here early today!"

"Here for something else now. We'll be back later for fish."

Jess understands Spanish better than she speaks it, but she manages "Quiero líquido" (I want liquid) that "hacer colores en comida" (makes colors in food). He understands and shows her the shelf, in the baking section, just like at home.

Jess takes the bottle and carries it to the cash register. She's about to pay when Maia brings over tortilla chips, salsa, and candy bars.

Jess looks at her with a raised eyebrow. Maia just looks back and says, "What? It's a party!"

Jess laughs and pays Mr. Díaz. Just as she picks up the bag to go, he adds a box of chocolate. He winks and says, "Have a good time!" in English.

* * * * * * * *

Aside from the slightly nauseating smell of the plastic (or is it from the bladder on the counter?), the girls are having a great time.

"This is so easy to use!" Maia exclaims, making her first bladder.

Emily agrees, "Yes, this printer is especially good. I like how we could put the dye right in with the filament, so it gets heated together as it comes through the extruder. Yes, this version is much better than the one I worked with in Pittsburgh a few years ago... they're really coming along."

Jess asks, "What did you make then?"

"A prosthetic limb for a dog my mom was taking care of."

"Aw..." Maia gushes.

Jess smiles, "I'm not too fond of plastic... the plastic in the ocean breaks my heart! But plastic limbs for dogs are ok by me!"

* * * * * * * *

After Jess has made her first bladder, she looks up from the printer and sees that they still have a lot of plastic filament left.

"Emily, I think we should make as many as we can. Who knows how many bladders are in that warehouse... maybe there are a lot more than three. And that way you'll have plenty for your work."

Emily nods. "I agree completely. Built-in excess capacity. Like building a bridge stronger than any load it'll ever carry, or having two kidneys when we only need one..."

"Or using three sentences when only two words are needed," jokes Maia.

Emily feigns a hurt look. In silence, she goes to the printer, looks dramatically at the other two, then hits the start command. As the flow of plastic begins, Emily grabs a piece... and flings a plasticene spitball at Maia.

* * * * * * * *

"Ladies, we've outdone ourselves. Those are eight beautiful totoaba bladders."

Jess says this from the couch, where she, Maia, and Emily are lounging after having gorged on snack foods. The bladders sit on the counter. Resting the stack of photos in her lap, Jess flips through the images, and looks up to compare.

"Yes, the shade is just right," Emily agrees, looking at a photo in Jess's lap.

"And the consistency... the just-a-little-bit-like beef jerky feel of it," agrees Maia.

Jess laughs and says, "We could almost sell these!"

Emily gets serious and says, "If warts take too long to come out... that might just be what we have to do. Flood the market with junk bladders... at least it would make the price come down."

The girls sit, quietly contemplating this.

Jess finally breaks the silence, saying, "Well, all good things must come to an end... this has been a lot of fun. But I think we all know what needs to be done next."

"A break-in at the waterfront?"

"A break-in at the waterfront."

* * * * * * *

Before the three girls leave the apartment, Jess asks, "Maia, where do you think we can find Cornelius? Do we need to go out to The Rock?" She asks this with some concern. Swimming out there takes forty-five minutes; they could fly, which would cut it down to ten, but she wants to draw as little attention as possible. And Emily can't fly, of course.

Maia understands her concern and shares it. "Yep, it'd be best if we could find him here in town... aside from the warehouse, we have to be in town to do our seafood buying tonight..."

"For your final Bird Feast!" Emily says eagerly.

"Hadn't even thought of that! I guess the birds will fly out tomorrow, huh?"

"With a little coaching from you, and a lot of coaxing from Mrs. B," Jess laughs.

"I think they'll be ok. They're getting pretty into it. Anyway, let me head outside and see if I can reach Cornelius by calling. It would save us a lot of time and effort."

"Let me just get these fake bladders into a bag, then we can all head out together," says Emily. She goes into the bedroom and grabs her backpack.

Maia stands up, none of them witnessing a yellow object falling from her lap. It lands in a corner of the room. A forgotten spitball.

The girls head out of the building; once they're a few blocks away, Maia starts shrieking in Gull, calling to Cornelius. After several minutes, she stops and says, "It's such a hot day... wouldn't surprise me if he's taking a nap in the shade somewhere."

"He deserves it, as hard as he's worked," says Jess.

Emily interrupts, "Hey, Maia, there's a common gull down the street. Why not ask him to help locate Cornelius?"

"Great idea." Maia screeches out again, this time a little more quietly since the bird is near.

The bird calls back to her, not bothering to come to her. In that heat, no one wants to do extra work.

Maia tells them, "He says he's about to fly to the beach, where it's cooler. I asked him to tell Cornelius to meet us at the harbor."

* * * * * * *

They head to the docks. As they're about to cross Tita's street, Jess says, "Tita must be dying for an update. It's Sunday, so the restaurant's closed. Let's stop by and see if she's home."

The others agree; after a few minutes, they're outside the Pérez house. Coco immediately comes to the window. To their delight, before they even ask, he nods, "Yes, Tita is here."

A minute later, Tita slips out of the house. She whispers, "Hello! What is happening?"

"We're going to steal some bladders! Want to come?"

Tita is torn. She wants to be involved, but she doesn't want to get in trouble. Plus, how is she going to explain this one? It's getting harder and harder to make excuses to her father.

On the other hand, her being there might be useful, in case they have to interact with any townspeople.

Before she has a chance to answer, María appears beside her. She looks at the girls with warm eyes and a smile, and says, "Go with your team, Tita! I'll come up with something to tell your father!"

"Stay, Coco." María holds him back as the girls run off.

* * * * * * * *

Once they're clear of Tita's block, the girls slow to a normal pace.

Jess discusses strategy as they go: "Maia, once we make contact with Cornelius, you two can be look-outs. Emily and I will do the actual break-in. Tita will stay nearby to deal with any locals."

When they reach the waterfront, there's no sign of Cornelius. Maia shrieks out to him. The other girls wander among the buildings, wondering which holds the prize.

After about ten minutes, and after Maia's made herself hoarse trying to reach the bird, the girls sit down on the sidewalk, wilting in the summer heat. Any other day, they'd be starting to worry: they have to get those bladders before they're gone. But the air is so oppressive it's hard to feel much of anything. Except Emily, who feels slightly woozy. Her eyes are a bit glazed, idly staring at a mark on the old gray plank wall in front of them. The bag of dummy bladders lies at her feet.

"I guess we should have brought some water," Jess remarks.

"Good idea," Emily says thickly.

Just as they're about to pick themselves up and head to the malecón business district to get something to drink, they hear a familiar squawk coming in from the sea.

"There he is!" Maia says with relief.

Cornelius flies in more lazily than usual. Once he lands, he talks with Maia more slowly than usual. Everything is taking much longer, as if the sun's rays had elongated time itself. After a minute or two... or five... Maia turns from the bird to the others and says, "Well, what do you know? It's this building right here... and he says he told me how to find it. I guess I didn't get the Gull completely right."

"'This building right here.'" Emily finally realizes what she's been fixated on. She says, pointing, "With an *X* made out of bird poop."

"Yep. *X* marks the spot."

* * * * * * * *

The heat makes it easy. No one's out at this time of day. Or if they are, they're out on pleasure boats that won't return any time soon.

Maia and Cornelius each fly to nearby roofs, and Tita takes position at the intersection of an alley and the street that lines the waterfront buildings. From there, she can see all traffic coming in.

But they don't need any of this. Jess and Emily encounter no danger at all, except for Emily saying, "Youch!" when she puts her fingers on the padlock. "Boy, is that hot!" she cries out.

Then she cracks the lock like an expert. Jess gushes, "Where did you learn that?!"

"Oh, that's an easy one. I learned it in Girl Scouts."

It's too hot and Jess is too tired to ask. She files it away under, "Must ask G about this some time."

She and Emily enter the warehouse, which contains several motors in various states of disrepair. There's an endless amount of rope and netting, some of it ripped, some just dusty from lack of use.

"Good thing I gave up on that net idea," Emily says.

Jess nods. So many nets in this place alone!

The warehouse is only slightly bigger than a shed, but it's crammed full. The sunlight doesn't penetrate the space well. In the dim light, the two bang their legs on boxes and tables as they explore the space.

"There's some shelves," Jess says. "Let's look at those."

Emily and Jess walk a few paces to the back, trying not to touch too much, worried that their presence will be discovered.

"What about that box?" Jess asks, pointing to a medium sized one on the top shelf.

Jess is too short to reach it, but Emily can. She pulls it down, and says, "It smells fishy... but so does this whole place."

They open it, and Jess says, "Bingo, my friend." She starts pulling out bladders: one, two, three...

"Those can't be the bladders from the other night," Emily says, looking at them as they pile up. "They're all dried out."

"No, but that's fine. Let's take out eight and put our eight inside."

Emily nods as Jess finishes pulling out eight bladders. "How many are left in the box?" asks Emily.

Jess counts them. "Seven," she says. Emily whistles: seventy-thousand bucks! And somewhere in the warehouse are the fresh ones from last night. And who knows how many others.

Emily holds her bag tight against her, to ensure they don't get confused about which are which. Jess takes the eight real ones outside, and sets them down at the base of the plank wall. Emily stays in the warehouse, and unloads the eight fakes into the box, mixing them in with the seven remaining real ones. Then she carefully restores the box to its position on the top shelf.

Trying not to bump anything else, Emily goes outside. Jess closes the padlock and twirls the combination, while Emily quickly loads her bag up with the genuine bladders.

Once the bladders are secure, Jess gestures to Maia on the neighboring roof. Maia calls over to Cornelius, "All clear?"

Cornelius shrieks back, "All clear!"

"Let's go!" Jess says.

Maia thanks the bird for his help, and flies down to walk with the others. Cornelius flies out to sea.

* * * * * * *

The four girls hustle away from the buildings and head to the malecón.

"That couldn't have gone better!" Jess says.

"Yes, the only problem we encountered was near-dehydration. Which was our own fault!" jokes Emily.

"I wish I had the keys to our restaurant! We could go there now," Tita laments.

Maia says, "Why don't we get a drink at Casa del Mar? They're always nice when I buy seafood."

It's one of the fancier restaurants in town, but they have a casual patio and it's only 4:15, so the hostess doesn't mind seating them. Despite their ordering only waters and juices, even the waitress is friendly.

"It's so nice to be under this umbrella," Emily says. "I was melting out there."

Jess says, "So, we're getting there, ladies. Tonight, Maia and I will hold the Final Feast for the birds. Tita, I assume you'll patrol as usual." Tita nods. "And Emily, you're going to test the solution, right?"

"Right. I have plenty of supplies for another batch of solution. And eight bladders are more than enough. I have to say, it makes me nervous walking around with a bag of those things!" As she says this, she uses her foot to push the backpack closer to her.

Jess nods. "Yep... $80,000 or so, huh? That's two or three years of college!"

"Or a restaurant here in town!" adds Tita.

Jess turns to her, "Do you think you'll take over your mother's restaurant someday, Tita?"

She nods, her eyes happy. "Yes, I think so. I don't want to leave."

Jess says, "No, of course not. Your family's here... your parents, and Coco..."

"... and the vaquitas!" Maia adds.

Jess raises her water glass, "To the vaquitas!" "To the vaquitas!" they echo, clinking their glasses.

* * * * * * * *

Jess pays the small bill, giving the waitress a large tip and a smile.

They exit the patio and stand together on the malecón. It's starting to draw crowds, people coming in for drinks and then dinner.

There's a feeling among the girls that they don't want to go. It's not the sluggishness of a few hours ago. They sense their mission is heading towards completion, and their time together is growing short. It's already been two weeks; Tita knows they won't be staying more than a month.

Impulsively, despite her shyness, she blurts out, "Thank you all! Thank you for coming to help me!"

Jess is the first to hug her and says, "Thank us? Thank you, my friend."

"We're all in this together!" Maia chimes in.

Tita hugs each of them, her eyes misting, then she pulls away. "I must go home."

"Who knows what your mom said to your dad!" Jess laughs.

"Right," Tita laughs. Then she turns to leave. After a few steps she looks back and says, "Tonight I'll tell the vaquitas all will be well." The other three smile and wave her on.

When she rounds a corner and is out of sight, Emily says, "Well, I guess I should go, too." She hitches the bag close to her body.

"Nothing to worry about, G," Maia says.

"I know. Just another day of carrying a bag full of fish platinum... such is my life..."

They all laugh and then she, too, departs down the street,

the backpack heavy on her skinny shoulder.

Jess turns and asks Maia, "You ready?"

"You know I am."

"Time to go shopping!"

* * * * * * *

As usual, they go to the grocery store first.

Jess greets the owner, "Hello, again." Even Maia throws in a shaky, "Hola... ¿Cómo está usted?"

Sr. Díaz asks how their party went that morning, then apologizes to Jess for being low on fish again. Jess won't hear of it. In her bad Spanish, she conveys to him: "It's Sunday, we're so grateful you're open at all. We know your shelves are pretty bare now... and it's our fault!"

They linger over his meager offerings. This will be their last time in his store. Aside from being fond of him, they realize he's never known why they come.

Maia pulls Jess into a corner where toiletries are stocked. Her eyes are filling with tears.

Jess says, "I know. It doesn't feel right, does it? I wish we could tell him."

They stand beside the deodorant and soap, welling up. Luckily, another customer comes in, so Sr. Díaz doesn't notice the girls' sudden disappearance.

After a minute, they manage to pull themselves together. They come out of hiding and complete the final raid on his freezers and shelves, then head to the cash register.

After Jess finishes paying, she starts to head towards the exit. Maia has already raced out, carrying her box. She can't communicate well with him and the feelings were getting to be too much. But Jess stops, and turns back to him.

She says, in the best Spanish she can muster, "This will be our last time here, señor. My friend and I want to thank you. We wish we could tell you what we're doing. It's to help the vaquitas. I want you to know that you have helped rescue the vaquitas."

171

He's just staring at her, kindness mixing with confusion.

"This town is very lucky to have you. All the best to you and your family."

After saying this, she bows low. Then she looks up, eyes red with tears, and gives him one last smile. Then she leaves, carrying her box.

* * * * * * * *

Maia and Jess head to the panga in silence, Jess pushing the cart with both boxes in it. A heaviness lies in the air, but it's not a bad heaviness.

Finally Maia speaks, "It's hard saying goodbye, isn't it?"

"You got that right."

Maia reaches out and touches her shoulder. In a more lighthearted tone, she asks, "To the panga?"

"To the panga!" They speed their pace a bit, energized.

"And then I'll head to the restaurants!" Maia says.

"Will you be ok alone? Your last time?"

"Yeah, sure. The staff at both have been friendly enough, but not like Sr. Díaz."

* * * * * * * *

EL JEFE

Tita tells me I do not need to worry any more. She and Jess... and there are others, she tells me... are making it so that the humans will not use the netzz. But she says we must be patient.

She has gone, back to the Coral Garden. Esperanza has been missing her, I know.

They are like sisters, those two.

* * * * * * * *

As Tita is enjoying a stressless "patrol" (really, a well-earned pleasure swim with Espy), Jess and Maia are setting the rock table for the last time.

"Come and get it!" Maia calls out in her lovely human voice. The frigatebirds have learned that much English Human by now.

Forty-five birds fly in, which has been the case every night, even though Maia had a discussion with their leader about who would travel to China. Only thirty will make the journey, but the frigatebirds look after their own. "Honor among thieves," Maia explained once to Jess.

Tonight Maia asks, "Are you going to take the panga back right away, or stick around?" Jess has been in charge of getting the boat back in place by early morning.

"Are you kidding? I have to be with these birds tonight!"

They're both looking out at the flock, affection overtaking disgust at their "table manners."

"They are slobs, aren't they?" Maia asks.

"Unbelievable." Jess says, then adds, "It's good they're going to fly out tomorrow, because I'm not sure they'll be able to hoist all that bulk into the air as it is... I can't imagine their getting any fatter..."

Maia nods, surveying the scene. "Yep, just call 'em Whale Birds..."

* * * * * * *

There's still plenty more to eat, but the birds have taken a pause. Jess sees it as a good opportunity to make a speech.

"Maia, tell them I want to say something to them."

Maia squawks at the group, who raise a chorus of answering squawks. Eventually, they quiet down, and Maia translates for Jess:

"I want to tell you that this is the last feast."

Unhappy cries greet that.

"Tomorrow – I mean, after the new sun comes..."

Annoyed cries answer her. They understand the concept of

173

tomorrow. What, does she think they're birdbrains?

"Sorry! TOMORROW – in the late afternoon, when it's cooler – we'll ask you to start your journey."

* * * * * * * *

As Tita is playing with Espy, and Jess and Maia are helping the birds, Emily is working away.

She cleans up the 3D printer, throwing away the excess filament and taking it to the dumpster outside. She boxes the printer up, thinking she'll arrange to send it back to The Agency.

Then, using what seems like every piece of glassware she has, she makes more solution. Once it's ready, she injects and coats the eight bladders with it.

She's about to scratch her right wrist when it dawns on her she's been doing that a lot... is her wrist trying to tell her something?

She peers down at it.

And then starts to laugh.

"Guess I wasn't as careful as I thought!"

* * * * * * * *

A little after dawn, Jess wakes. Maia is sleeping soundly, and a few feet from her, most of the frigatebirds are sleeping, too.

"They really trust us," Jess notes with satisfaction, and a little pride.

As quietly as she can, she heads down to the water's edge. She can feel his bark wanting to escape, but she beats him to it, whispering, "Good morning, Sammy!" With the same poignancy she felt toward Sr. Díaz, Jess realizes their time together is growing short. Jess doesn't think Sammy could ever understand what he means to her. But she tries: "You know, Sammy, I know a sea lion up in California..."

Sammy barks back, albeit more quietly than usual.

Jess laughs, "You're right. This *is* California. But I meant the state of California, about three hundred miles from here... anyway, his name's Simon and he's a friend of mine... He's sick right now but when he gets better, maybe you could meet him some time."

Sammy barks his approval at the idea.

She says, "You could swim together... or lie on my board together..."

Then a series of barks hits her, and Jess knows he's arguing about that pronoun. It's *his* board.

Ooh... there's an upcoming confrontation that she doesn't relish.

Ignoring it for now, and trying to restore the morning's peace, she whispers, "Gotta go, my friend." Then she hops into the panga as quietly as she can and says, "See you later, buddy!"

* * * * * * *

After she returns Miguel's boat to its spot on the beach, Jess heads to the restaurant. Emily is already there. And both of them have arrived before the Pérez women.

"If we had a key, we could get to work!" Jess jokes.

They begin to tell each other about how their nights went. Jess is trying to follow all the scientific terms flying out of Emily's mouth when she catches sight of her wrist.

"What happened? Did you scratch yourself?!"

Emily laughs sheepishly, "Just a victim of my own plan."

Jess gives her a confused look.

"Poison ivy."

* * * * * * *

They're still getting caught up when another customer comes. Jess recognizes him as Pedro, the guy that was there her first morning in town.

He seems anxious but manages a "hello" which is neither

175

friendly nor unfriendly.

Jess and Emily attempt to act like two tourist teenagers looking for breakfast; when Tita and María arrive, they give their "orders" and they all pretend not to know each other. María seeks solace in the kitchen, wanting to escape the awkwardness.

Pedro orders his meal and doesn't even notice that his food comes out before that of the two girls who were ahead of him. In fact, he's so preoccupied he also doesn't notice six eyes staring at him as he eats, wishing him away.

He finally finishes and gets up to pay. Tita nearly jumps to the register. "Anything else, Pedro?"

"No, thank you. See you soon I hope, Tita."

When he leaves and is definitely out of earshot, she turns to the other two and asks, "How was it? Are the birds ready?"

Jess nods, "Yep, today's the day – we're thinking around 5:00."

"Good, I will leave work a little early and join you." Then Tita asks Emily, "And were the tests ok?"

"Everything looks great. The bladders haven't changed at all. When I left they looked as fresh as when I started. The solution's stable."

Jess asks her, "And the supply for the birds? Is it ready?"

"It's all divided up; I just have to transfer them into new tubes. They're smaller – better for the birds."

Jess asks, "Do you need any help?"

"No, shouldn't take too long. Besides, I don't want anyone else to risk warts... or poison ivy."

Tita looks to her, obviously not familiar with the term.

Emily extends her wrist and lifts the bandage. "It's a rash you can get from the plant, *Toxicodendron radicans*."

"Ah! La hiedra venenosa!"

"I didn't realize you had it here," Emily says, embarrassed by not knowing something.

"It is not common here. But my cousin had a bad case after visiting Cabo San Lucas. Her eyes were swollen shut."

"Well, we have it all over our back yard... you might say,

this rash is a gift from my mother!"

"I take it she doesn't know why you wanted the plant?" Jess asks.

"No, but let's just say she supports my pursuit of knowledge."

* * * * * * * *

More customers start to arrive. Emily and Jess eat a quick breakfast, anxious to free up the table.

"Tita, let's meet at the boat rental at 4:00," Emily says, pretending to pay at the counter.

"Ok, see you then," says Tita, pushing the bill back at her before walking back to bus tables.

The two girls step outside and onto the sun-filled promenade. Jess looks out at the sea. "I wish you could come with me today, G. It's wonderful, being with the vaquitas. They're so charming and graceful. And it just feels... *right* to have them here. The sea is happy. You can feel it when you're with them."

Emily listens, interested but not envious. "Maybe I'll learn to swim, and come back to swim with Tita."

"Yes, Tita would love that! And the vaquitas would, too. I know she's told them you're helping them. You know, G, if it weren't for you and your Idea... your crazy solution... they wouldn't survive."

Emily gets a little flustered, for once not knowing what to say. After a moment of embarrassed silence, she simply says, "See you at The Rock."

"At The Rock! 5:00! Don't forget the goods!"

* * * * * * * *

Near the end of the work day, Tita asks her mother to make excuses if she doesn't come home for dinner. She isn't sure how long she'll be gone.

"Tonight's the night, hmm?" asks María, her eyes shining.

177

Nodding, Tita embraces her, then leaves. She walks to the beach, happy in her thoughts. Wanting to enjoy the warm sand, she bends down to take off her shoes. A ball comes rolling towards her feet.

"Tita!" Juan Carlos cries out, chasing the ball, happy to see her.

"¡Hola, Juan Carlos! How is your summer going?"

"It's good... there haven't been any vaquita deaths all month, did you notice?"

Tita smiles and wishes she could tell him. All she says is, "I think things will be ok." Then she gives him a hug and hands him his ball.

She finishes walking to the stand, where Emily's waiting, a bulging satchel hanging from her shoulder.

Sr. Ramírez doesn't even bother to ask for a note from María. He hands Tita the key. She thanks him and asks what time's the latest they can return the boat.

"Normally sunset, which tonight is about 7:00. But, for you, Tita, it's ok if you have it back by morning. Just be careful, yes?"

"Thank you, Sr. Ramírez. But I hope we will have it back in time."

He smiles, thinking to himself, "You might have it back in time... but how many people will be with you? Seven? Eight?"

* * * * * * * *

Emily pilots the boat out with confidence. "That's very good, Emily," Tita says as her friend brings it in gently to the base of the island.

They disembark, and get a bark: Sammy saying hello.

"Do you ever move, Sammy?" Emily asks him.

"Hola," Tita says gently, resisting the urge to pat him. Unless it's a vaquita, or Coco... or an orca... she thinks it's best to leave wild animals alone.

They clamber up, Emily carefully tending to her bag.

"Welcome, ladies!" Maia smiles, making a sweeping gesture

178

as if inviting them onto a red carpet, instead of a poop-laden rock face. A gesture that indicates: This is the place to be.

A few of the frigatebirds have already arrived. Their preening and fluttering add to the sense it's opening night on Broadway. The air is full of nervous anticipation, the hope that everyone will perform well and it will all go successfully.

Taking it all in, Maia says, "Jess should be here any minute..."

"Did you notice? She's only minutes late these days... not hours..." Emily and Maia joke about their friend.

"I heard that!" Jess says, coming up from finishing her patrol.

"How are the Area Eight?" Tita asks. She can't believe she still hasn't met them.

"Good. They seem happy these days. I think even they can sense things are on the move for them."

* * * * * * *

Maia gathers the others to her. This is her night. She starts by saying, "Ladies, I gotta be honest: if anyone had ever told me I would get fond of smelling like shrimp and sitting on a bird poop mountain, I never would've believed it!"

They all laugh and Jess chimes in, "I even like these selfish birds!"

Maia smiles, and as she looks over the ones already gathered, her mood grows more serious. They're asking a great deal of these animals. It's an exhausting and potentially perilous journey.

"Time to begin," Maia says, and turns from her friends and shrieks into the afternoon sky.

The frigatebirds there join in her cries, and a symphony of squawks begins, as the birds call to bring in their kin. Eventually, forty-five birds settle on The Rock.

Maia begins: "Thirty of you..." But she's met with earsplitting screeches.

She makes a gesture for them to quiet down, then says to

179

the largest bird, "What is this, Captain Fairbanks?"

She clacks back and forth with him, then explains to the girls: they all want to go.

"I only made thirty vials," Emily protests. But Maia holds a hand up to her, as if to say: no need to argue with them. These guys stick together.

She resumes, "The forty-five of you will fly across the Pacific. You'll be in two groups but will stay together. At the very end of the journey, the two groups will part ways. I've already talked with your leaders and their lieutenants about this. Alpha Company will go to Hong Kong. Beta Company will go to Guangzhou."

The frigatebirds listen and they understand everything except "Hong Kong" and "Guangzhou."

The humans listen and they understand nothing except "Hong Kong" and "Guangzhou."

Maia says to the birds: "I've reviewed these locations and their landmarks with your leaders. They know where to go."

Then Maia bends down and picks her phone up from the ground. She starts the call with a quick greeting, introducing herself to Lynn Chang.

Then she squawks, "Alpha Company Captain Fairbanks and Lieutenant Penzy, please come here."

The two birds approach. Maia bends down to hold the phone so they can see the screen.

"This is your contact, Commodore Lynn Chang. Memorize her voice and face."

There – the birds can't understand the magic of it – is a human face calling out to them. The accent is not the same as Admiral Maia, and her skin is not brown but very pale, and her top feathers are not curly black but straight black. But there is a human calling out to them in Seabird, telling them where to meet her at Hong Kong Harbor. Telling them she will have a feast waiting for them, congratulating them on their fine appearance, their strong flying. And promising them it is the most sacred of missions.

This is repeated with Beta Company Captain Redthroat

and his second-in-command, Lieutenant Talbot. Again, Maia holds her phone to allow a young Asian woman to speak to them in Seabird. She tells them precisely where to come in Guangzhou. Commodore Mei Li is not as fluent as Commodore Chang, but she manages to flatter them, and promises a feast.

Captain Redthroat and Lieutenant Talbot expand their throat sacs, then salute. "Count on us, Commodore," clacks Redthroat.

A shiver goes up Emily's spine, and it's not a cool evening. She feels it... her crazy plan is about to take off – literally! And it's going to work!

The other girls are getting excited, too. They never saw these Asian bodhis before. It's so nice to know they're not alone.

Maia hangs up with Mei Li, and her eyes are gleaming.

"Officers, please come here." The four hop in close.

"If you're agreeable, I would like two of you to wear this small box on your backs..."

Fairbanks, Redthroat, Penzy, and Talbot are all eyeing up the contraption that Admiral Maia holds out. It's a little box with a shiny surface and something that looks like a small stick protruding from it.

Fairbanks looks at it greedily. Won't he look handsome in that?! He grandly turns and offers his back.

Using special glue, and with gentle but firm fingers, Maia clamps the GPS tracker to him. Fairbanks spreads his wings and jiggles side-to-side. The device stays put, the gray antenna bobbing with his movements. Impressed with it and with himself, he clacks and puffs out his throat.

Redthroat screeches his displeasure: why is Fairbanks always first? He pushes the lieutenants out of the way and offers his back. Once the device is on, he and Fairbanks vie for who can wiggle the antenna more.

Penzy and Talbot squawk unhappily. But to the leaders go the spoils. For all the honor of their titles, they're just footbirds.

Satisfied, Maia stands up and says to the captains, "Well, now that we have some extra birds, you two won't need to carry tubes as well as the transmitters." She turns to the birds at large and says excitedly, "So... all that remains is to load you guys up."

"Load us up?!" Penzy squawks inquiringly, and not very happily. Captain Fairbanks joins with him, showing his camaraderie (though he can't help but think the antenna must look especially good with his vigorous bobs of protest.)

"Forgive me, my Seabird still isn't fluent. I used the wrong term. I meant: give you the tiniest thing to carry..."

And, in fact, the burden is not huge: just two grams for each bird. Two grams of a solution that Emily hopes will end the totoaba trade for good. A tiny burden... but every bit will be felt on a seven thousand mile journey.

Captain Redthroat shrieks in displeasure. They were not told this!

The girls feel bad. They certainly never meant to hide it from the birds. To them, it seemed obvious the journey would involve carrying something.

The other frigatebirds start talking amongst themselves, shrieks and screeches as the news spreads. Maia tries to appeal to their vanity – after all, they wanted to carry the antennae, didn't they? But it's to no avail. "Wearing something" and "being loaded up" are just too different. Maybe it's a nuance of the Seabird language. In any case, they want nothing to do with the vials.

The whole thing is coming dangerously close to unravelling. Maia starts to worry she'll have to get Mrs. Bixby involved again, when Jess steps in, shrieking.

The others look at her in amazement.

The birds fall silent.

Jess musters all the grandeur that her five feet three inch frame can manage, then shrieks and shrieks.

Maia just shakes her head. Tita and Emily stare at each other, wondering what Jess is saying.

The birds stare at her, and Jess starts to flap her arms. Her shrieking continues, and soon she is soaring fifty feet above them all. She hovers there for more than a minute, the glorious late sun shining behind her, making a halo around her light brown hair.

Finally, she lands gently. Not a sound comes from the birds, the girls, or even Sammy down below.

Jess says to Maia, "I think that should do it."

Maia just gapes at her.

Jess continues, "But please translate this for me: You are truly noble, self-sacrificing creatures…"

Maia translates…

"…'magnificent' does not begin to describe you!"

Emily is hurriedly getting the little vials strapped to their backs before they can re-consider.

Captain Fairbanks squawks one final time, but then nods his head and bobs the antenna sharply to Jess. As if to say, "You're right."

* * * * * * * *

Tita asks Maia what Jess said to the birds.

"As far as I could tell, she made no sense at all. It was just a lot of noise."

* * * * * * * *

Once Emily has completed her work, and made sure the tubes are evenly divided and securely on, Maia reviews the troops. She makes it clear to the birds that Jess is their Supreme Commander. Maia doesn't mind ceding authority – clearly, Jess's power is the only thing getting them to do this.

With a final clattering of approval, Maia salutes the companies and gestures to the western sky. One by one, the birds take off, heading west over the Sea of Cortez to cross the thin Baja Peninsula, then over the mighty Pacific.

Impulsively, both Maia and Jess leap up after them, escorting them out. Circling and watching nearby, Cornelius flies to catch the group. In Seabird he cries out, "Brothers, thank you! Protect our sea!"

* * * * * * *

On land, Tita is astonished to see Emily start sobbing. Tita goes and sits with her, trying to comfort her.

"I hope it will work!" Emily says, looking very young.

"I have faith in you," Tita says.

Emily calms down and looks out to where the birds are now only visible as dots. She laughs and says, "And in those birds."

"Yes. And in those birds."

* * * * * * *

After a few minutes, Maia and Jess fly back in, with Cornelius. He doesn't land on The Rock, but cries goodbye to the girls, and heads off to be with his flock.

Maia and Jess can't hide their tears. In fact, all the girls feel it: an odd mixture of elation and concern. But Jess shakes it off and rallies them. It's a night for celebration!

She gathers them in a huddle. Then she cries, "Here's to Emily for coming up with The Solution!"

"Here, here!"

"And here's to Maia for training those birds!"

"Here, here!"

"And here's to Tita for holding down the fort so long all by herself!"

"And for bringing us together!" Maia adds.

"Here, here!"

Then Emily says, "And here's to Jess... a leader I'll follow wherever she asks!"

"To Jess!" "To Yess!"

A bark from Sammy comes up from below.

* * * * * * *

The birds have started their journey. Do they make it?

Does Emily's warty idea succeed?

Will Anita's beloved vaquitas be saved?

Read the exciting conclusion in *Vaquita Days*!

AUTHOR'S NOTE

I started working on this book in early 2015, and the population estimate I first heard was one hundred vaquitas. A year into the project, the estimate was down to sixty, and I had to change some book details to match the reality. Then in March 2017, I learned that the latest estimate was thirty vaquitas. This news was so disheartening that I almost gave up. But after a few weeks of feeling hopeless, I came to the conclusion that more people knowing about the vaquita could only be a positive thing – if nothing else, maybe their tale will help us prevent another animal's extinction. So I got back to work, changed the manuscript again, and decided self-publishing was the quickest way to get the story out there.

As I prepare to go to print, August 2017: the Mexican government recently declared a permanent ban on gillnets in the vaquitas' waters. It also announced a plan to employ dolphins (trained by the U.S. Navy) to herd the remaining vaquitas into a safe area, where hopefully they can breed.

Dolphins herding vaquitas?! That's almost as crazy as frigatebird couriers. Here's hoping the plan succeeds!

I invite all readers to follow not just my story, but the real story. And if you're able, consider donating to an organization involved with conservation efforts. A few of these include:

Sea Shepherd Conservation Society
Viva Vaquita
Greenpeace USA/ Greenpeace México
Porpoise Conservation Society
World Wildlife Foundation
Pronatura Noroeste

ACKNOWLEDGMENTS

Thank you so much to my early readers: MEG, Judy Goodhart, Warren Hoppe, Anneliese L, Maureen Puskar, Diana Roberts, Sarah Roberts, Iris R-B, Kate W, Sage W, and Tasman W. Thanks and love to my H/G family, The Friends, Bert, and Sissy. Thanks to Angelo Baiocchi, Amanda Godley, and Paula Hoppe for all their amazing help. I'm also very grateful for the professional advice of Patrick Flores-Scott, Marah Gubar, Becky Tuch, and Siobhan Vivian. More thank yous to Laurie Cohen, Patricia Donohue, Helen Dorra, Kathy Fifield, Carl Hammer, Jona Hammer, Benjamin Hicks, Amy Krawczyk, Nancy Lardo, Karen Lautanen, Michael MacKenzie, Roger Rouse, Matthaeus Szumanski, and Theresa Webber for their kindness and encouragement. And thank you to the Grub Street Writers' Conference in Boston, which is a fantastic resource in just about every way.

Finally, thank you to the many people and groups trying to help the vaquitas. The ones I've personally encountered are listed below. My apologies to all those I've missed, especially the scientists and reporters who have truly told the story of the vaquitas.

Aidan Bodeo-Lomicky/ vlogvaquita
Sea Shepherd Conservation Society
Viva Vaquita
Greenpeace USA/ Greenpeace México
Porpoise Conservation Society
World Wildlife Foundation
Pronatura Noroeste
Leonardo DiCaprio Foundation
Carlos Slim Foundation
Marisla Foundation
Mexico's Secretariat of Environment and Natural Resources
U.S. Navy and Navy-trained dolphins
Creators and crew of the film *Souls of the Vermilion Sea*

ABOUT THE AUTHOR

Like a vaquita, S. H. Goodhart is a shy creature. She would much rather hear about you than talk about herself.

But she knows Emily is not the only curious soul out there, so here are a few facts about her:

-she loves all animals (no surprise there!)
-she often "patrols" her neighborhood, picking up plastic trash to protect waterways and sea life (don't be a litter bug!)
-she is a practicing physician (it's a privilege to care for people, but not as much fun as writing this!)
-she lives in a black-and-gold city (same as two Bodhi Sisters!)
-she can surf, but not very well (Jess should give her a lesson!)
-this is her first book (thanks for giving it a look!)
-she has great faith in you (please help take care of our beautiful planet!)

For perhaps a few more details about the author, but definitely a lot more about the vaquitas (and how to help them), please visit the website:

www.vaquitadays.com

But don't stay online too long.

Get outside. The Earth is waiting for you. ☺

78441562R00120

Made in the USA
Columbia, SC
16 October 2017